TRAIL OF THE ORACLE

JACK GANNON

CYNDI WILLIAMS-BARNIER

YBR Publishing
PO Box 4904
Beaufort SC 29903-4904
contact@ybrpub.com
843-900-0859

ISBN-13: 979-8-9852082-8-3

YBR PUBLISHING, LLC

Jack Gannon – Co-Founder, Production Manager
Cyndi Williams-Barnier – Co-Founder, Production Editor
Bill Barnier – Senior Editor
Loreen Ridge-Husum – Art Director

"It is the strange fate of man, that even in the greatest of evils the fear of the worst continues to haunt him."

~Johann Wolfgang von Goethe

REVIEW

Reviewed by Alma Boucher for Readers' Favorite, LLC

"Trail of The Oracle" is a mystery murder by Jack Gannon and Cyndi Williams-Barnier. Lieutenant Commander Angela Jason, also known as Agent Oracle, is the agent in charge of the Task Force's (digital) section, which conducted a specialized study on the internet and the dark web. Angela had a natural aptitude for using her imagination and spatial judgment and could search through data streams for concealed data. A few weeks ago, Angela found a Goliath cipher, which indicated that there was a terrorist threat. Angela identified Mister Terrence as a terrorist. Mister Terrence reported to someone that he made sure he was seen on his way to Washington and that the Task Force was hunting him. When students die and Mister Terrence suddenly disappears, it cannot be a coincidence, and a special team is deployed to investigate.

"Trail of The Oracle" moves quickly and is filled with mystery, intrigue, and suspense. Jack Gannon and Cyndi Williams-Barnier took me on an unpredictable ride full of twists and turns that I never saw coming. This book was an absolute page-turner and kept my eyes glued to the pages. I was captivated from the start until the end and could not put it down. I could never predict what would happen next, and I was kept guessing throughout. The characters were well developed. They were surrounded by mystery, and each had a code name. Angela was my favorite character. She was steadfast and gave her all to get answers. The story was excellently written with an intricate plot. I enjoyed it and recommend it to anyone who likes reading murder mysteries with a cyber slant to them.

ALSO BY THE AUTHORS

The Task Force Series
2s And 3s
The Task Force That Saved Christmas
Trail of The Talon
Trail of The Hunter
Bite of The Black Widow

The InSpectre Series
Dawn of The Living Ghost
Tears of Destiny

Others
I Walked in Santa's Boots: Lowcountry Christmas Memories
Tales on The Yellow Brick Road 2023 (Anthology)

TASK FORCE DIVISION

A specialized federal agency created by the Pentagon to solve the unsolvable…

CHAPTER 1

DISCOVERY

Regardless of the time, the offices of the Task Force Division were always open, as all departments operated across the clock, gathering information of potential threats to the United States from across the Earth. The information was distributed to the appropriate departments or sections within the complex.

One office group, however, did special research within the confines of the internet and significantly the dark web. The agent in charge of that group was Lieutenant Commander Angela Jason, code-named "Agent Oracle". She was a natural spatial savant, allowing her to look at data streams and find hidden information that was otherwise impossible to detect by standard research or even special algorithms.

Her position was unique in the Task Force hierarchy; she was an active-duty Naval officer on permanent dispatch to Task Force. She arrived in uniform daily, but on the rare occasions that required her to do field work she would wear the standard form-fitting black uniform with knee-high black leather boots, elbow-high black leather gloves, and a leather gun belt which contained the tools or additional ammunition which the mission would require her to have on hand. She wore a narrow set of black glasses which were also a data receiver to display to her eyes-only special information her belt sensors might detect, as well as a tactical assistant assigned to her at the division headquarters.

Like every field team agent, her gun belt buckle was a flat non-reflective metal; engraved on it was her agent symbol, the symbol of ancient alchemy: a circle in a square in an equilateral triangle in another circle. Her current weapon of choice was a Glock. She was a naval pro-marksman.

But tonight, she was engaged on a particular hunt in her data streams: she had recently caught sight of a planned murder, but beyond that she could find nothing. Even her data team, some of the best in the country, could find no corroborating data points for follow-up.

Angela sat at her desk, a steaming cup of coffee in her left hand as her right moved the computer mouse back and forth to highlight lines of code on her 40-inch desk monitor. "Where are you?" she said to the terminal. "Come back to mama."

One of the overnight Task Force staff stopped at her open office door and knocked gently. "Commander?" he asked.

"Enter," Angela replied. A young naval ensign, also assigned to Task Force division due to his high scores on the special boot camp graduation test, entered and saluted. She returned his salute without rising. "Speak," was all she said.

"Commander," he began, "we have a screen lock for you to see."

"Pipe it through."

"If I may?" he replied, pointing at her terminal. Angela scooted back in her desk chair to allow the ensign room to slide behind her desk and enter special codes on the keyboard. Her live data stream was replaced by a static image from the master memory cache. He pointed at a sixty-one-character long stream of figures. "This raised flags on three different researchers' screens, "Commander," he said.

"Very good, Ensign—" she glanced at his nametag "Bernard. How long ago was this capture?"

"Four minutes, seventeen seconds," Bernard replied, looking at his watch.

She looked at him sternly. "You could have just called me, Ensign."

"Yes, ma'am," was all he said.

She turned her attention to her screen. "Son of a gun. That's a line of Goliath." Angela looked at Bernard. "Do you know what the Goliath cypher is, Ensign?"

"No, ma'am."

"I wouldn't expect so. I only discovered it a few weeks ago, hasn't even been circulated to the researchers. Sit down."

Bernard took a seat on the other side of her desk. "Since you've now seen it, I will be advancing your security status. Eyes Only, Under Penalty." She opened the file drawer of her desk and brought out a folder with only a couple of sheets of paper in it. "This is Goliath." She handed it to him.

He accepted it and opened the first page. His eyes widened after reading the first paragraph. "Commander, is this what I think it is?"

"You got it, Ensign," Angela answered. "We have an active terrorist threat on American soil..."

CHAPTER 2

PLAN

Ensign Bernard asked, "And just what is our next step, Commander?"

"Second page." He looked at the second page in the folder. "That contains my personal algorithm for looking for that cypher in the data streams. Since I didn't know what we were looking for until we found it, I've been writing back door codes for any cypher I could find. This is not a copy-and-paste code to apply to that line of code; it has to be keyed in manually—"

"—and within thirty seconds?" he interrupted. "Ma'am, I'm good, but I'm not that fast."

"I know that. Nor am I. In fact, no one on staff is fast enough. But I'm going to set off a 'time' bomb to buy you another thirty seconds. Can you do it?"

"I, uh," he began to answer as he looked at the thirty lines of code on the page, "I can do it, ma'am. But, if I may ask, why can't you do it yourself?"

"The Goliath is a well-crafted code," Angela said. "But, in order for me to set off my bomb to buy extra time it will begin backtracking to my IP, which means I have to spend that minute building new redirects every couple seconds, and it can't be one of the ones I've built in the past. Goliath is practically intelligent on its own, and it will follow the live signal back to its source…and we don't want it tracking back to me. While I have it distracted, you'll be able to use the interact sequence to add my code, which will allow us to then follow whatever Goliath does."

"Just asking, ma'am…what is the penalty part? Not that I plan to do anything, of course."

"Very simple, Ensign." Angela leaned forward, interlacing her fingers on the desk. "Say a word about this to anyone, except to me or the captain, and you'll spend the rest of your natural life in solitary confinement. The Goliath code could very well launch us into a nuclear war."

"Holy, crap…ma'am!"

Ensign Bernard sat at his desk in the research cubicle area of Angela's department, headset on so only he could hear her instructions. "I'm going to give you a signal on your phone to start entering that code, and you'll have 59 seconds to complete it. Are you ready? We'll have only one chance at this. Tap your phone line to me if you are." He tapped at the line on their connected call. "Okay, I'm going to hang up and when you see the phone light flash on your end start typing as fast and accurately as you can. No mistakes, no backspacing to correct. Ready?" He tapped the button again. "Okay, counting down from five seconds… Mark." The line disconnected and he watched the time on his computer screen, and at in five seconds he began typing the code Angela gave him. Wisely, he had placed a sign on the back of his desk chair reading "Do Not Disturb For Any Reason".

In her office, Angela began keying furiously, creating international signal misdirections to keep Goliath from discovering the Task Force complex. She ignored the desire to check the time, concentrating on creating bounce points across Europe and South America, plus a couple in the United States to keep from looking like it was a U.S. infiltration.

Bernard and Angela typed furiously.

At 55 seconds Angela received the signal that Bernard was finished. She created a lock location in Tehran. She sat back, balling her hands into fists and extending her fingers until Bernard reentered her office without knocking. "Did it work?" he asked.

"Only one way to find out," she said. She created a new external link to enter the Goliath stream without using the same IP address. Once in, she needed only a few seconds. "Yup, we're good and we're safe. Excellent work, Ensign."

"Thank you, sir," he said.

She cocked an eyebrow at him.

"So, if I may ask, what was this 'time' bomb?"

She smiled again. "It was a time displacement code. Made a second last two seconds. Any longer than a minute would have set off alarms. Less than a minute can seem like an internet disruption like we have from time to time."

"Ingenious. Now what?"

"Now, we wait for my time worm to work…"

CHAPTER 3

BRIEFING

TEN MINUTES EARLIER

Captain Mark Jason, U.S. Naval Reserve, CEO of Jason Enterprises, and leader of the Task Force field team, arrived at the Task Force complex outside Washington, D.C., for the weekly mission brief. After entering, he set his attaché on his desk, followed by a corpsman with a cup of coffee. Finally ready, he sat at his desk and placed a video call on his computer.

Within seconds the face of a grizzled older man with a white crew cut appeared. "Good morning, sir," he said in a muzzled growl.

"Good morning, Sarge. I trust all is well this morning."

"Had a couple kids try to deface your artwork in the front plaza."

Mark smiled. "I trust you…disciplined them properly?"

"They'll be writing again…in a few weeks," Sarge Brunson, his security chief, deadpanned. "All else is good here, sir. I assume you're settled at the DC office?"

"Of course. I do miss not having Ellie with me this week. My personal secretary means the world to me, you know."

"She does get vacation time."

"When she's forced to take it," Mark replied. "Heading to briefing with the black suits, will check in later."

"Aye, sir," Sarge said, and Mark disconnected the call.

Mark's assistant at Task Force, Lieutenant Junior Grade Abigale Cutter, knocked at his office opening, as the door was still withdrawn in its wall pocket. "Good morning, Cutter. Enter." The young naval officer entered and handed him a tablet. "Feels heavy," he jested. "I take it there's a lot for the briefing?"

Getting his joke, she smiled before answering. "Quieter week than the usual, Captain," she said, standing at attention.

"At ease, Lieutenant. Sit down."

Cutter sat across the desk from him. "It remains a difficult situation at the border, sir. We've already got a couple million illegal immigrants in the country—"

"—which is outside our charter," Mark interrupted.

"Yes, sir, but it's the number of terrorists that have been intercepted trying to enter from Mexico. Mathematically there are a lot that have gotten through into the country."

Mark sat back in his desk chair. "Do you have stats or educated guesses?"

"Well, both, sir. We're pulling from every camera across the southern states, and dispatching feds when we lock on a target and locate."

Mark stabbed a finger at the tablet to look at Cutter's report. The room was painfully quiet, but Cutter was used to Mark's habit of deep concentration. However, it was when he looked up at her while his face was pointing down that she felt her heart skip a beat. "Is this verified?"

Without asking his reference, she said, "Aye, sir."

"Son of a bitch," he grumbled. Again, the office was silent as he ran plans through his mind. "I want you to attend this morning's briefing, only to listen."

"Aye, sir," she said, understanding their conference was over and standing to offer a salute. Mark returned the salute with a "Dismissed" command.

As Cutter left, Mark pressed a button on his side console. "Briefing Room One, five minutes."

Four minutes later Mark was in the briefing room closest to the Task Force team's offices. He sat at the head of the table, with Division Director Tom Michelson to his left. Tom was a retired Marine, half a foot shorter than Mark. The remaining team members entered and took their seats: Calvin "Seeker" Geffers, Harri "Proteus" Lewis, Mae-Lei

"Hunter" Kamala, and new member Stephanie "Firebrand" Anderson.

Precisely five minutes since his gathering call, Mark said, "I see that Angela isn't here this morning. Is she in her office, Cutter?" he asked his assistant behind him.

"I haven't seen her this morning," Cutter replied.

"Hm. Probably caught in her matrix world again. Well, anyway…I have a report that an old friend of ours is out and about with a new contract."

"Who might that be, Mark?" Hawaiian-born Mae-Lei asked.

"The Talon."

"Mother Fu—" Calvin began to say before Stephanie elbowed his ribs. He winced slightly before adding, "Sorry about that."

"No problem, Cal," Mark replied. Calvin and Stephanie, when she was an FBI agent, had captured The Talon years before in Argentina after stopping his plan to assassinate the American Ambassador. "But there's some question on this report: his escape was just sent to us, but it also indicates he had escaped way back during the Black Widow affair?"

Calvin reflexively put his hand on his neck. That was where the serial killer known as The Black Widow had injected concentrated Latrodectus venom into him so she could escape capture. "Bad memory," he mumbled, "even after all these years."

"Understood. But we're not going after him."

Calvin's eyebrow went up. "Come again?" the black man asked indignantly.

"Sources indicate he subcontracted an out-job to do an execution."

"Sounds like him," Stephanie answered.

Harri, the shortest team member whose hair was short spiky platinum blonde, asked, "So, do we know who the subcontractor is?"

"Funny you should ask," Mark replied. "It's your job to find him."

Harri, the team's technical expert, said, "I thought you were gonna give me something hard to do this time."

Mae-Lei smiled. "Smartass."

"Rest of me is still cute, too."

"Okay," Mark interjected, "back on task here. Harri, you're on research. Cal, Mae, you two are on capture, so prep Cal's car for immediate departure and remain on standby. Coordinate with Harri for direction as soon as she has directions. Also contact Joint Base Andrews to prep a transport just in case."

"Roger," Calvin answered for them both.

"Steph, get with your FBI allies, do the routine searches. See if any of their CIs have some underworld info."

"You got it," Calvin's blonde wife and former FBI agent said.

"Okay, team, dismissed. Let's get this person before he or she hits whoever the target is. Cutter, go by Commander Jason's office and tell her to report to mine immediately."

"Yes, sir," Cutter replied, and followed the other team members out of the briefing room.

"Not a word from you today, Tom?" Mark asked the director when they were alone.

"Nah," he said with a smile. "Just enjoy watching you run the show."

Mark also smiled. "Not like I haven't been doing this for, what, a dozen years now?"

"How you've done both this and run your international company all this time…I think I'd've been put in an asylum by now. How do you do it?"

"That's easy, Tom," Mark said. "The people know their jobs and duties, both at Jason Enterprises and here at Task Force. I just give them their assignments then get the hell out of their way."

"I knew that," Tom said. "Come see me after your meeting with Angela. Got something special for you."

"Sure thing." Mark stood, tablet in hand, and left the briefing room.

Cutter was waiting for him at his closed office door. "Captain?"

"Go ahead," Mark said.

"She's on her way to your office, sir."

"Thank you. Follow me." She accompanied him into his office and sat across from his desk when he directed her to do so. He sat in his executive chair and waited for Angela to arrive. "Come in and sit down, Lieutenant Commander," he said when she was at his open door.

She knew she was in trouble when he addressed her by her full rank. "Aye, sir," was all she said as she sat, her tablet in her left hand.

"I don't care if you are my daughter; when I call a full staff meeting, I expect you to be there."

"Aye, sir."

He sat back in his chair. "Don't 'aye, sir' me," he said with a smile. "Now that I chewed your ass as required, Angel, what kept you away?"

"I tracked a terrorist threat already here."

"The Talon," Mark said.

"Nope."

Mark and Cutter both looked at Angela. "Not Talon?" Cutter asked.

"Oh, he's out and about again, no question. Does not seem that there's any prison that can hold him, and I'm working on that part. No, what I mean is that we have a new player here."

She confirmed what he already knew. He sat forward, fingers intertwined on his desktop. "Talk."

Angela tapped at her tablet. "This player is all but a ghost. I've been able to connect some of his hits internationally, but only because one of the targets had access to Goliath and didn't complete a code entry within his time limit, which alerted one of my dark worms—"

"Spare me the Star Trek technobabble, Angel," Mark said, tilting his head gently. "Give me the bottom line."

"You never say that to Mom at JE," Angela poked back.

"Ha, ha."

"I got a name, or, rather, part of a name."

"Which is?"

"Terrence. Mister Terrence."

"That's it?"

"That's it for now."

"That matches information I got from my own sources," he said. "Always good to have confirmation."

"And how is this Mister Terrence to be considered a threat?" Cutter asked. "And which Mister Terrence across the globe would he be?"

"Great questions, Ensign," Angela replied. "I've got Bernard working in my universe, searching around."

Mark narrowed his eyes. "I assume you gave him verbal authority?"

"Aye, sir," she answered. "The paperwork has been processed and is on its way to your desk any time now."

"Very good," he said. He sat back and focused his eyes on the wall between and behind the women.

Cutter leaned over to Angela. "He's planning something now,

right?” she asked in as light a whisper as she could.

Angela wordlessly winked at her. Cutter sat back and waited with her for him to address them again.

After a minute he leaned forward and pressed a button on his phone. “Hunter,” Mae-Lei responded.

“My office, now, please.” He then said to Mae-Lei, “Get Bernard in here, too, if you would.” He rose and moved to the multi-seat discussion areas of his office, inviting Cutter to accompany him. Angela joined them after calling her assistant.

Mae-Lei and Bernard arrived only seconds apart at his open door, both saluting. “Come in,” he said, returning their salutes from his desk. “Mae, seal the door please.”

She complied, and she and Bernard sat on the open couch spots.

First Mark said, “As of this moment, the five of us, plus Tom and the other field team members, are the only ones to know what we discuss in this office. We will be the only ones to be involved in this mission, which means that tactical support will not be involved in anything we do. Bernard, Cutter…you will be our support.”

“Aye, sir,” they answered in unison.

“Commander,” he said to Angela, “please brief the others on what you’ve already told us.”

Several minutes later Angela completed updating Mae-Lei and Ensign Bernard. She concluded, “Now that you’ve all been brought into knowing about Goliath, any discussion of it with anyone not authorized by Captain Jason will be tantamount to treason with possible life in solitary confinement.” She smiled another rare smile. “Of course, that goes without saying that I know none of you would do that.”

“You had to say it,” Mark added. “Mae, I’d like you to set these two up in one of the top secure surveillance rooms and tie their coms to our frequency. This is a Dark Mission. Then dress and meet us in the parking garage.”

Everyone except Angela departed without being dismissed. She turned to her father. “You said ‘us’?”

“Well, what are you waiting for? An engraved invitation?”

Angela knew she was going to participate in one of her rare

Task Force field operations. "Aye, SIR!" She did a smart about-face and nearly ran to her office to get into her field uniform, leaving her father chuckling at her enthusiasm to do something besides read the dark matrix…

CHAPTER 4

CHECK-IN

I have reached Position Knight," Mister Terrence said into his cell phone. Terrence, a muscularly bulky black man in a three-piece suit, continued in his English accent, "I made sure I was tagged at the southern border as directed. No problem getting to Washington, made sure I was seen the entire trip. He and his team are no doubt on the lookout for me now."

"Excellent," said a soft German-accented male voice on the phone. "You will continue as ordered."

"Yes, sir," Terrence answered, and disconnected the call. Placing his phone in his inside jacket pocket, he grabbed his bowler from the bureau and placed it on his head as he exited the hotel room.

Amanda Curry loved working the afternoon shift at the restaurant. It was between the lunch and dinner rushes and allowed her the few extra seconds with the midday diners. She kept her dirty-blond hair in a ponytail and wore only light makeup when she wore her blue waitress uniform dress. She was a single mother, currently not dating, and so was focusing her attention completely on her customers.

She held her breath when the black man in the gray three-piece suit and dark gray bowler entered the front door. The only sparks of color on him were his white shirt and red rose on his lapel. Amanda thought he was the most beautiful man she had ever seen. "Table for one?" she asked in an almost-raspy query.

"Yes, please," Terrence replied.

Amanda felt her heart skip a beat in excitement. "Right—right this way, sir," she stumbled, and immediately kicked herself for not staying professional. She led him through the mostly-empty dining room to a table booth for two. "Will this do?"

He smiled. She swooned in her mind again. "Perfectly," he replied gently. "Cup of Earl Grey, please, if you have it?"

"Absolutely," Amanda said, and she departed for the kitchen. *Damn damn damn...he is so HOT!!!*

Terrence casually glanced around the open area to confirm there were security cameras while he pretended to peruse the menu. When Amanda returned with his tea, he said before she could ask, "I'd like to try your house grilled cheese, with baked beans and coleslaw." He took a sip of his tea. "And I forgot to request honey."

Did he just call me honey? "Oh, HONEY, yes, absolutely...and I'll get your order in." *Get your act together, Amanda!!!*

He sat quietly until she returned with the honey bottle. "Anything else while your meal is being prepared?" she asked.

"Not...yet," Terrence replied. He doctored his tea as she stepped to the kitchen and awaited his lunch. He said softly so his ear comm would pick up his words, "Have arranged Target One."

"Execute as you wish," said the German voice into his ear.

His lunch arrived only a few minutes later. Terrence told

Amanda, "Thank you. May I have another cup of tea?"

Amanda smiled. "Of course, sir," she said. *God, his voice is so magical!* "Be right back." She returned a minute later with a fresh steaming cup. "Anything else, sir?"

"Ah, thank you, no. Just plan to enjoy this American pastime." She nodded and stepped away, looking back on her way to the front desk to wait on a couple who had just entered. He ate his lunch while watching Amanda seat the new diners and dutifully tended to them as she had him. He ate his lunch unhurriedly, enjoying the entire meal more than he'd expected.

She watched him frequently, returning to his table as he was on his last couple bites. "Would you like some dessert?" she asked.

"Thank you, no," he replied with a gleaming smile. "Check, please."

She removed the order wallet from her apron. "I can pick—"

"Don't go." He placed a fifty-dollar bill in the open wallet in his hand before reaching into his pocket to put a small plastic envelope in the wallet with the money. He closed it and handed it back as he rose from the table. "Keep the change. Have a wonderful day." He took her right hand in his left and gently kissed the top, then picked up his bowler and headed for the exit.

Amanda stood there feeling completely flushed…

CHAPTER 5

SHARING

What's this, Mom?"

Amanda looked at her seventeen-year-old daughter, Dagen. "What's what, dear?"

The brunette-haired teen picked up the little plastic bag from the counter next to her mom's purse. "This?"

Amanda looked over from her sink of dirty dishes in the kitchen. "Oh, that's just something a guy gave me at the restaurant. Left me that instead of a cash tip."

Dagen looked at the contents in the clear little bag: a business card with a graphic on it, along with a matching charm and gold chain. "This card has a bird claw on it. Matches the gold charm."

Her mom nodded her head as she continued rinsing off the dishes and placing them in the dishwasher. "Yeah, I saw that, too." She sighed.

Dagen heard the sigh. "You like him?"

Amanda dried her hands and joined Dagen at the counter, saying softly, "Oh, my, God, He was SO dreamy! Big muscles, British accent—"

"British?" Dagen interrupted. "I love him already! Did you get a name, phone number—"

Amanda signed again. "No, darn it. And he paid with cash."

Dagen said softly, "A dad with a British accent. OMG…"

That made Amanda look up at the mantle over the gas-powered fireplace. In the center was a picture of them with her late husband, who died in a firefight in Iran. Dagen saw where her gaze went. "It's been three years, Mom. I'm sure Dad would be okay with you being attracted to someone new."

Amanda began to flush. "I don't know what it was, it was like he was sending me pheromones or something…he was SO GORGEOUS!" She felt her face get hot. "Oh, my…"

Dagen laughed. "You are so into this guy!"

"Not the kinda topic I should be discussing with my daughter," Amanda whispered as she walked back to the sink. "You are too young for this conversation, young lady!"

"Yeah, yeah, yeah," Dagen replied. "You tell anyone else? Maybe Sandy or Estelle—"

"No, no one at work knows. It was the slow time after lunch, and they were on their own break. I had recovered myself before they got back."

"Uh, huh."

Amanda glared at her daughter. "Uh, huh, what?"

"You are dying to tell them!"

"Tell them what? That a customer got me all excited—" Her eyes went wide.

"Oh, my God, Mom! You were so turned on!!!"

"I was not!" she protested…but only momentarily. "Well, okay, maybe a little."

Now Dagen was laughing and blushing.

"People your age should not be thinking that kinda stuff!!!" She started laughing again.

Amanda shook her head, smiling. "Oh, Lord, what are you doing to teenager's minds these days?"

The doorbell rang.

They stopped laughing.

"You expecting someone?" they asked each other in unison. "No," they replied together.

"Well, go see who it is," Dagen suggested.

Amanda dried her hands off again and dropped the towel on the counter. Dagen accompanied her to the front door. Amanda looked through the peephole to see who the caller was. Her mouth dropped, and Dagen asked, "So, who is it?"

"Um," Amanda started, slightly shaking…

CHAPTER 6

GUESSING

S on of a bitch!" Whenever Mark heard Angela cuss it was because she couldn't solve a problem, which was rare. It was also why he ordered her to keep her office door open so he could listen for anything. He pressed the phone line to her office. "Yes, Daddy?" she answered.

"Come over here," he said gently, and closed the line. By the time she reached his office he had two tumblers on his desk and a bottle of Scotch in one hand, filling each. He offered her one filled tumbler and raised the other in his free hand. "Cheers," he toasted.

"Cheers," she replied, still tense. She licked her lips after the first sip. "Love Glenfiddich."

"Same here. Love that first little burn before everything goes numb from the tongue to the tummy."

She took another sip. "You are definitely the world's best dad. But when you told me to get dressed in the field uniform, I thought we'd be on the road immediately."

He was dressed in his black uniform, same as her. His gun belt, gloves, and full hood lay on the corner of his desk, while she had her gun belt already fitted over her waist and strapped to her right thigh. "That's because when I say it's time to move, I don't want to waste time changing clothes. So, who's the guy?"

"I was able to trace his travel to Centreville, but then he dropped off the grid and out of the dark matrix. It's like he just faded away."

"That's an hour from here," Mark commented. "That tells me he's coming to DC."

"I agree. But the 'why' is out of reach."

"For the time being." Mark took another sip and looked at his glass. "Although I know we shouldn't be imbibing right now, you needed a fast relaxant."

"Where's the chocolate?"

Mark smiled as he pulled a box of chocolate truffles from one of his desk drawers. "Yup, just a little extra sugar to the body to help digest and process this medicine faster."

"So, this Talon person. I've read up on everything we have about him. If he escaped during the Black Widow affair, why are we only learning about it now?"

"That's a question I'd like the answer to as well. For now, though, we concentrate on this Terrence fellow. Got anything on him yet?"

Angela's eyebrows furrowed. "It's like he's a damn ghost. But, he's a black ghost, at least."

"Come again?"

"Black. Dark skin, black hair. That's as much description as we've been able to gather."

"That's it?"

"I'm pissed because that's ALL I've gotten after all these hours. Bernard's got nothing, either."

"So, we have a new player on our board," Mark said gently. He sipped his Scotch, then stared at the glass. Angela watched him quietly, not moving, for a few minutes. She could see in his eyes the concentration as his trained military mind was running scenarios.

"Centreville was the last place he was detected by city cameras," she finally muttered. "But on a direction to DC." Another minute of silence.

Finally, he stabbed at a black button on his phone bank. "Field team, to my office, on the double."

◆

"He wanted to be seen coming this direction," Mark revealed to the team. "Not explicitly so, but just enough to send enough dark web alerts to reach us when he was ready to be seen."

"The mystery is still 'why'?" Angela added.

"My gut is telling me it's something big," Mark continued. "The mystery is 'what'."

"And 'where' and 'when'," Harri piped in.

Mark nodded in affirmation.

"Obviously it's something here in the Capitol," Mae-Lei said. "Why else would he come straight this direction?"

"Unless that is a misdirection," Calvin answered. "We're to think he's coming this way to do something here specifically, when perhaps the target is—"

"Angela," Mark interrupted. "Get in your boards. Look for the word 'target'."

"Aye, sir," she said, as she darted out of his office and into hers. She was back in only a minute. "You pegged it. There is a communication line listing a 'target' was contacted."

"But not who specifically?" he asked.

"Not that it helps much," Angela replied. "Just someone or something identified as 'Target One'…"

CHAPTER 7

MISDIRECTION

T his is…quite a surprise," Amanda said, trying hard not to stutter in his presence. "Um, customers aren't supposed to follow employees' home," she added as professionally as possible. Although her door was still chained, she doubted it would stop someone his size from breaking in.

"My sincerest apologies," he said, smiling. "I was walking this direction from a meeting a block away and saw you come into this building. Curiosity got the better of me, I'm afraid…you were quite the dear one when at the restaurant, I wanted to say thank you again."

Dagen mouthed to her mother from behind the door, *"Oh, my God! I love his accent!"* That drew an eye roll from Amanda.

Returning her attention to the unexpected visitor, she continued, "Well, um, thank you very much, but again this is really not appropriate."

He removed his wallet from his inside jacket pocket and removed several folded bills. "I failed to leave a monetary tip in addition to that tiny gift." He offered it to Amanda. She took it from his large dark hand carefully so as to not have her hand be grabbed. "I shall take my leave and not bother you again…except perhaps the next time I dine on your watch. Have a wonderful evening." He tipped the brim of his bowler and stepped away.

"Wait!" Amanda called out. "Um, what, um…what is your name?"

"Mister Terrence," he replied with another smile and pressed the elevator button. Silently he waited for the door to open and he stepped in, Amanda watching the entire time.

She closed the door, forgetting the folded bills in her hand.

"So how much?" she heard Dagen ask.

"How much what?" Amanda replied.

"Tip?"

She finally remembered the money in her hand and looked down. Her jaw dropped when she counted the cash.

"Well?" Dagen asked again.

Amanda sat in the armchair of her living room set, her daughter on the sofa end closest to her mother. All the bills were spread across her lap. "I just don't…!"

"Is it real?" Dagen asked.

"Sure looks real enough," Amanda answered. "I just never…I mean, this is SO MUCH…!"

"What did you do for that guy?" the daughter asked. Amanda started to scowl to make her say, "I don't mean THAT way!!! I mean, any special treatment or such?"

"I just waited on him, that's all!" They both sat staring at all the cash in Amanda's lap. They had both counted it out to the same amount. "But ten thousand dollars? As a tip? For a simple lunch?"

"I know, right?" Amanda lifted one bill from her lap. "But a in hundred hundred-dollar bills?" She lifted another. "They're not brand-new, they don't have consecutive numbers…all different years that I can tell. So not a ransom payment—"

"Getting paranoid, Mom?" Dagen asked.

Amanda smiled. "Maybe a little. But, you always come before anything else. If this is real money, then great for us, and thank you, Mister Mysterious Terrence. Tell you what; I'm off tomorrow, so let's go to the bank and have a couple of these checked. I'll pick one, and you pick one, so both will be completely random. If they're both good…then yippee!"

"Can I go with?" Dagen asked.

Amanda shook her head. "You're still in school but come home quick instead of going to Sara's. Deal?"

"Deal!" She rose to her mother's seated form and gave her a hug. "Nighty, nite, Mom. I love you!"

She patted one of her daughter's arms around her. "Love you, too, little bug. I'll see you in the morning." She watched her precious daughter walk down the apartment's hall to her bedroom…then cast her gaze down at all the cash on her legs…

"Both real," Patti said from behind the teller's station upon reviewing the high-dollar bills. "You got quite the tip!"

"He was quite the customer," Amanda confirmed.

"So, what did you do to earn—"

"Oh, not you, too?" she said mockingly. "First Dagen, then you? Is it really THAT strange of me to earn a bigger-than-ever tip at work?"

The brunette Patti replied, smiling, "Well, at THAT place, maybe!"

"Ha, ha," Amanda said, "Thank you, dear, I appreciate you checking for me. One can never be too careful, now."

Patti extended her hand to Amanda, returning the bills, their fingers lightly brushing together in the exchange. "You did the right thing! So go spend it and don't worry about it!"

◆

"Nothing new after twenty-four hours?" Mark asked the team.

"Sorry, boss," Mae-Lei answered for the team. "This one is proving to be tougher than usual.

"Angela, anything new in the dark?"

"Not a damn thing," she said, using her father's favorite saying.

"Harri, Cal, Steph, anything in your contact worlds?"

They all shook their heads "no".

Mark took a full circle walk in the conference room. They were all dressed in their black uniforms, and all but Mark was armed and ready to move out when ordered. Bernard and Cutter sat in corner chairs, silently observing. He finally stopped in front of the room's large flatscreen monitor. "Angela, put the border video up." She entered commands on the keyboard. The screen came alive with a view of one of the border areas of the United States with Mexico, showing views of all the drivers and occupants in the cars entering from the southern country. "Side screen, predicted entry time of this Terrence." She split the image in half, projecting a map of the southern border with a calculated map of Terrence's journey across the country.

"Best estimate…around 8 a.m. Monday."

"Program into the search parameter body recognition rather than facial. We don't know what he looks like…so let's try a broader approach. Someone, and we are safely assuming a man, who looks out of place entering the United States at a legal border crossing."

"Out of place?"

Mark smiled. "Yeah, with the tens of thousands crossing the border every month these days, it's like looking for a needle in hurricane debris."

"This will take a while," she said.

"To run?"

"To set."

Mark sat in his seat at the table head. "Everyone on standby, go back to your networks and search for anything. Cutter, three coffees, please."

"Aye, sir," she said. She knew what to get Mark and Angela, but asked, "Who gets the third one?"

"That's yours. Make it quick, we've got research to do, and I have no idea how much time we have for what we don't know…"

CHAPTER 8

FRUSTRATION

Angela rubbed her eyes. Even for a prodigy like herself, too much concentration on one thing for a long time was tiring. She sat back in her desk chair and sighed. "Before you say a word, Daddy, the answer is still 'no'."

"That's 'Captain Daddy' to you, Angel," he said, trying to elicit a little levity in the situation. It landed so badly that Angela could only groan with her eyes still closed. "But, I know, this is the most complicated thing I've ever asked you to find."

"He's like a freaking ghost," she grumbled, Mark knew his daughter was beyond furious when she tried to cuss.

"When's the last time you slept?"

"When what?"

Mark stood up from the second desk in her office where he had been attempting to help. "That answer tells me everything. You've got a bed in the back, get some sleep."

"But—"

Mark glared at her with the look she'd known since her childhood, and she knew the battle of words was lost before it began.

"Aye, sir," she said with a gentle salute.

"I'll wake you if there is anything…anything at all," he said.

"Thank you." She put her arms around his neck and gave him a soft kiss on his cheek. "I love you, Daddy."

"I love you, too, Angel," he replied with a gentle kiss back. He waited until her private room door closed at the rear of her office before he left the main area; the pocket door automatically slid closed.

As he took the few steps to his office at the end of the Field Team wing of the Division, he realized that he was starting to feel the fatigue of his long hours as well. When he sat behind his desk, he pressed the direct lines to every team member except Angela and said, "Team, everyone is ordered to get some sleep. Set all your searches on automation with an order to wake you if anything is detected. Sleep well." He did not wait for any answers, as he went to the bed in his own office's back room…

◆

Patti Simmons settled at her teller station to begin counting her till drawers, taking a sip of coffee as she picked up the first stack of bills. She savored the flavored black coffee, this morning as a K-cup of French Roast.

She finished counting the single-dollar bills and placed them in their slot, picked up the loose five-dollar bills and prepared to count them on her countertop. Patti took another sip of coffee…and her vision rapidly faded, her teller station swirled in front of her, and rapidly she fell backward in her teller stool, all the way to the floor, her full coffee cup flying away to the side and her five-dollar bills tossed into the air before settling on and around her. The other tellers screamed in surprise and ran to her, plus the bank manager.

Blane Jackson, the bank manager, had also been a Navy

medic before retiring and entering the financial world. He quickly checked her pulse and breathing before saying softly, "She's dead!"…

CHAPTER 9

INVITATION

N ot a damn thing," Angela said again. She raised a fist to smash into her keyboard but thought better of it and gently lowered her fist to her desktop. "How's that, ma'am?" Bernard asked.

"Nothing. Go back to your research." Angela turned to her interoffice intercom and pressed her father's direct line. "You busy?" she said into the speaker.

"Come on over, Commander," she heard her father's voice reply.

She said to Bernard as she left her office, "You know where I'll be—"

"Yes, ma'am," he replied as she walked out of her office and the pocket door closed behind her.

She approached her father's office door, but it slid open as she neared. The interior lights were all off, and she entered the blackness without hesitation. Angela stood silent as the pocket door slid closed, leaving her enveloped in complete blackness save for the flashes of light that developed in her eyes.

Angela knew this environment well. Whenever her father

needed to concentrate this deep, he needed total darkness. He would normally also cover his ears from sound, but knew he needed to keep that sense alert. She could only wait for him to end this round of deep thinking…

◆

"How was school today?" Amanda asked Dagen when she got home from work.

"It was ok," her daughter replied. "Just another day of filling my head with mush."

Amanda took her daughter in her arms for a comforting hug. "It's not mush, little bug," she countered. "It's no different from going through your closet to find the right combination of blouse and jeans and shoes for a date; you may not need it all right now but you will eventually."

"Wow," Dagen said as she backed away. "That was, like, real profound!"

"Not bad for a parent, eh?"

Dagen giggled. "Yeah, not bad."

"So how much studying you got tonight?"

"Uh, profound parent, it's Friday…no homework, remember?"

This time Amanda was the one to giggle. "Oh, yeah. I'm sorry…just had a really busy day. Payday and all. Despite so many doing direct deposit these days, there are some who still do in-person deposits, and I really like that."

"Any stories to share?"

"No, nothing exciting today. You know, it kinda felt like a gray day." Amanda began removing items from the freezer and refrigerator in the kitchen to start preparing dinner.

Dagen glanced out the window. "It's sunny out."

"No, gray as in it was just a yech day."

"That time of month?"

Amanda admonished her with a furrowed brow glance.

"That was last week, and it doesn't last two weeks. Guess I was just tired today and didn't want to be there."

"Why didn't you just call in sick?"

Her mom sighed. "Despite that we're ok with my salary and what your dad left us, I just like going to work and seeing people every day. COVID just really ruined so much for me…"

"Wow, if that's what I'll be experiencing when I'm your age I'd rather not be your age!"

"Ha, ha, smartass. Now get off your butt and set the table."

"What's for dinner, by the way?"

Amanda smiled evilly. "Crow…"

Dagen was in her homeroom, settling in for roll call and morning announcements. She noticed her friend Sara was not yet in her seat.

"Good morning, students," came the principal's voice. "This morning I wish to convey some sad news. One of our own passed away last night: Sara Carey. She fell ill last night and passed away at the hospital. Let us take a moment to remember her—"

Dagen looked at the empty seat beside her. "No!" she said aloud in shock, drawing attention from her classmates and her teacher, who immediately made her way to the distraught student.

"—and counsellors will be available for anyone wishing to speak to them. That is all; classes will commence as normal."

Mrs. Eskill bent down gently as Dagen rose to her feet, crying and reaching out to be held. The students in the classroom were all shocked; girls cried and held each other, boys talked to each other about Sara, some with wet eyes and others who knew her better also cried.

Ensign Cutter entered Mark's office habitually as she would on the days he would be at the Division offices, not braced for the total darkness and Angela's tall form blocking the entrance. Fortunately, Cutter not only kept the coffee from spilling but also stayed on her feet after backing up from Angela. "I'm so sorry, sir," was all she could say.

"Lights," Mark said. Once the office lights were at normal brightness, Angela sat unbidden while the ensign stayed at attention at the open pocket door. "Cutter! Why did you enter without acknowledgement?"

"Sir, one of your first orders to me when I was assigned to you was strong black coffee at o-730 hours. It is o-730, sir."

Mark looked at his watch, confirming the time. "My apologies, Ensign. Remind me to instruct the commander to teach you about some of my other...unusual habits. So, let's have it." He extended one hand with two fingers curled to accept the coffee cup by its handle. "Now that I'm awake, do you have any updates for me?"

"No, sir," answered Cutter. "This target just does not show up in any databases."

"I concur with the ensign," Angela added. "It is like we're searching for a ghost that never lived but walks among us."

Mark knocked his knuckles on the desktop as he sipped his coffee with the other hand. "Alright, Angel, we gotta think completely differently. Cutter, with apologies, get out."

"Aye, sir," she replied as she did an about-face and left the office.

Angela eyed her father blankly. "What was that about?"

Mark only sipped at his coffee a few more times. A minute later he said, "Go get the rest of the Field Team."

She knew when she was ordered to physically gather the rest of the team, he needed a few more minutes alone to think and plan, so she simply nodded affirmatively and left his office.

He steepled his fingers in front of his face and closed his

eyes, looking deep into his personal darkness.

In the hallway, Bernard met them only a couple feet from Mark's closed door. "Speak," Angela told Bernard…

CHAPTER 10

SHARING

Dagen had asked to be picked up from school, and her mother arrived from the restaurant as quickly as she could. Amanda found Dagen in the nurse's office, still crying. After checking her daughter out of school for the day, she walked her to their car and drove home…

After Dagen settled on the couch with her favorite comfort blanket, Amanda stepped to the kitchen and returned a minute later with two wine glasses, offering one to her daughter. "Sip this," she said.

Dagen looked up with wet eyes. "You always tell me I'm too young for wine yet."

Amanda sat beside her and clinked her glass with Dagen's. "It's for medicinal purposes this time."

"Wait, I know that line." She took a light sip.

"Dr. McCoy from Star Trek."

Dagen smiled. "I knew that." She sipped again. "This is good!"

"Pinot Grigio. My personal favorite." Dagen sipped again. "Slowly, little bug, slowly."

"Yes, ma'am."

Amanda paused for another sip herself. "So, Sara passed away? I didn't know she was sick."

"She wasn't. I was just with her night before last, she was perfectly fine, she was fine at school yesterday morning, and then—" she began to tear again.

Amanda held her close with her free arm. "It's okay, baby, it's okay…you just cry as much as you need…"

The silence was broken only by the sound of sipping and crying…

Doctor Trevor Nolan placed his Franklin-style reading glasses on his desktop and closed his eyes as he stretched and yawned. It had been a long day at the Fairfax Memorial Hospital on the border of the Town of Centreville with several victims of automobile accidents, two shootings, a broken leg from a school sporting event, and one severe illness.

The illness stymied him; he could not match the symptoms to a specific illness, and in the end, he had to intubate the patient in intensive care. He referred his findings to the Center for Disease Control and was awaiting a return call.

When he opened his eyes a solid black figure sat in front of him, a woman with long black hair wearing black lensed glasses and a black body suit. Around her waist she wore a leather gun belt. "Who—who are you?" he demanded.

"Calm down," Angela, in her full agent guise of Oracle, said gently. "I'm no threat; in fact, I can be a friend, if you let me."

Seeing that while she was armed but not holding her

weapon on him, he began rotating his arm to the alarm under his desk. "Don't bother reaching for the button; I've already deactivated it."

"Are—are you going to kill me?"

She smiled. "If I was going to kill you, you'd already be dead."

Trevor began to slow his breathing after understanding the logic of the moment. "So, if you're not here to kill me—"

"I'm going to be straight with you, and I what I tell you stays in this room. Breathe a word to anyone—and that includes trying to turn on your recorder remotely—would make a very unhealthy thing occur to you. So, are we on good terms?"

He nodded.

"Good. I'm a special federal agent on a priority assignment. There's a suspected terrorist in the country, and I'm running all databases through my matrix, looking for anything at all that might help me…and then your patient lit up my alarms. What have you got?"

"Oh. Well, Miss—"

"Agent Oracle."

"Agent Oracle…she's exhibiting signs of flu and pneumonia, as well as appendicitis, yet when I test for them all there are no physical infections. What's certain is that she is dying, and I have no idea how to treat her. Right now, I have her on oxygen and an IV drip while I search for answers."

"May I see your tests and patient?"

"Are you a doctor?"

She cocked her head in an "are you serious" angle. "Just take me to her…and clear the halls first." She rose from her seat, looking at the unmoving physician. "That was not a request."

Moments later Trevor was guiding the tall black-clad woman to his patient's room. He opened the door for her to enter first, but she instead motioned for him to precede her. "We don't need company." He lifted her chart from the bed foot and handed it to her. "Any suspicion of COVID?"

"No," he said. "As you can see—"

"Asymptomatic of influenza and pneumonia, with abdominal bloating…but no diarrhea or flatulence. No fever. No respiratory issues. Temperature normal, blood pressure normal…" She flipped to the computer monitor of her primary functions. "Pressure 100 over 73, pulse 65, temperature 98.7." She looked at the woman…actually, a teenager, after a quick glance at the chart… "So, why isn't she out picking up boys?"

Caught by surprise with the question, he grinned but quickly returned to a serious face. "I don't know yet. Outwardly she severely symptomatic; inwardly, she's perfectly healthy."

"And the edema?"

"The tests show she's in severe danger, her nerves weren't responding to standard tests, yet the MRI shows perfectly normal."

Oracle returned the chart to the doctor and stood silently, staring at the young patient. "Please put her in an induced coma and keep her that way until you hear from me."

"You can't give me—"

She turned to him and stared at him; even with her eyes covered he suddenly felt very small. "I'm telling you what to do to save her life. This may be part of something bigger, but I admit I'm not sure. For now, excessive caution is the rule. And should you get any other patients in here with matching symptoms, do the same procedure as you have on…what is her name again?"

"Tabitha. Tabitha Galiene…"

By the time Trevor looked back at the chart to answer the question, Oracle was already gone from the room, as well as the hospital floor. She had secreted her way down the stairwells jumping from landing to landing in her cushioned boots until she reached the garage and her Division car. Once behind the steering wheel, she said aloud, "Tactical, Oracle. Please tell me you got all that."

"Copy, Oracle," said her assigned support technician at Task Force Division. "All data has been encoded to research."

"Coordinate all findings, if any, to Ensign Bernard exclusively," she ordered.

"Aye, aye, Oracle. Any other orders?"

Oracle sat silent for several seconds. "Not a damn thing right now…"

CHAPTER 11

CHASING

Mae-Lei Kamala and Calvin Geffers, otherwise known as the Hunter and Seeker of the Task Force Field Team, arrived in Centreville, Virginia in the late morning. Their dark car windows kept people from staring in to see their high-tech dashboard and computer systems as they sat in their cars of the Lion Run Elementary School. "Tactical, Seeker, requesting update."

"Seeker, Tactical. No update. Maintain station per Spy. Out."

He and Hunter were parked driver-side to driver-side. He rolled down his window, and she did likewise. "I guess from your sour face that there's no update."

He replied, "Yeah, no. I hate waiting."

"Tell me about it, Inigo," she replied, referencing "The Princess Bride" character. "Not like all our assignments are complete action and adventure."

Seeker chuckled. "So true. But frankly, I don't mind easier assignments these days…"

"Oh? Starting to get old on me, old friend?" She pointed

at her temples, indicating the solid white temples in his otherwise black hair.

"Ha ha," he said. "Your caramel skin will never look as tasty as mine."

"In your dreams," said the Hawaiian agent to her black partner.

"Hold on," Seeker said, as his attention was pulled to a readout on his dashboard.

"Whatcha got?" Hunter asked.

After a few seconds, Seeker replied, "Medical dispatch from Oracle. Lotta stuff I don't understand, but apparently no firm leads."

"Well, shit."

"Language," he said, "in case any youngsters come out while we're here."

"We should be here at night."

"We can't always be hidden by the dark," said Seeker.

"I just don't wanna be watching for kids," replied Hunter.

"Know the feeling."

"So, now what?"

Seeker punched a couple buttons on his console. "There's another elementary school a mile or so away. Go there and stand by."

"Righto." Hunter rolled up her window and left the parking lot.

Seeker changed his radio frequency. "Spy, Seeker."

Mark's voice came across the private channel. "Seeker, Spy."

"We got anything to work on?"

"Nothing," the team leader replied. "Oracle is following up on new dark network files, but nothing actionable."

"Well, lovely. Anything I can do while we keep waiting?"

"Take a pass along I66 and up to Dulles, see if anything catches your attention. I'll dispatch other agents to other streets."

"Roger," said Seeker. He put his car into "drive" and took

off for the nearest interstate access.

Angela entered the Field Team offices and went straight to her father's office. The door slid open before she could knock, and she entered without asking, and sat without receiving permission.

Her father was on the other side of the desk, conducting his own computer searches to which only he had access. "Please, come in and sit down," he said without looking up.

"Not feeling humorous, Daddy," she said.

"I better see a smile, or I'll kick your ass," he replied, "and you know damn well I'm the only one in this command who can actually accomplish that."

She tilted her head and nodded, a small smile emerging on her lips. "Well, that much is true."

"I taught you everything you know, but not everything *I* know."

"I know."

They both smiled.

Angela pulled down the zipper of her one-piece uniform front and added, "This thing needs to be redesigned and upgraded."

"We're trying to find an invisible terrorist and you want to talk work fashion?"

"Do you realize how much the girls are squeezed in this thing?"

"Not like I spend time looking at my own daughter's assets."

That made Angela laugh. "You're the only man I know who can say something about his daughter's body parts without breaking into a sweat."

"I remember going out with you and your mother to find

your first training bra, and you being so excited to try it on in front of me and—"

"Oh, God, don't remind me!"

Mark chuckled. "I'm making you blush! My all-business-face daughter is blushing!"

"Oh, stop already!!!"

"I cannot wait to tell your mother!!!"

Their gaiety was interrupted by a notification beep on his computer. Angela rose and walked to his side. "What do you have?"

"First Responder report of another student passing away under suspicious circumstances."

"Where?"

"Centreville."

She checked her portable monitor from her belt. "I got nothing from my auto trackers."

Mark pressed a button on his phone. "Hunter, Seeker, twenties."

Two lights popped up on a map window that appeared on his screen. "We've got another death. You're both too far away. Oracle and I will handle this one. Out." He rose from his desk seat, grabbing his gun belt with a four-sided diamond emblem etched in the flat metal buckle and his full head-mask. "Grab your gear and follow me."

"We're intervening in a police matter before we're called? Why?"

He looked at her as he buckled his belt around his waist. "Let's call it a professional hunch."

"As in…?"

"A terrorist disappearing in Centreville…and a student death in Centreville. Could be a coincidence."

"But you don't believe in coincidences," she said, nodding.

Only a couple minutes later they were both in his black car, roaring out of the Task Force garage…

"Police are still on scene," Oracle said as their car neared Sky View High School in northern Centreville.

"Put your badge on," Spy told Oracle.

She opened her buckle front panel and removed the federal badge that she placed over her left breast. "Don't you forget either, Daddy." He nodded and complied. With his full head mask on she could see no facial expression. But despite knowing who was under that mask, she was still slightly shaken when he looked at her. *Damn, but he's good! Gotta be the shape of his eye lenses...*

They both exited his car and walked quietly into the school, offering no communication with the police on duty. They were met by a female police sergeant at the entrance. "We received the order to clear the area for you," she said, extending her arm to guide them to their right. "Third room on the right."

Spy stopped in the doorway and visually scanned the room, the mini cameras in his mask lenses recording everything he saw. By the wall was the still form of a female student under a window. He focused his gaze on the floor. He saw nothing out of the ordinary. "Go," was all he said to Oracle.

She entered and advanced professionally to the girl. She knelt beside her head and placed her equipment bag by her foot and began removing several black devices. Spy remained in the doorway to keep people from entering while Oracle began her work.

One device, a black cylinder, was placed on the girl's neck; it took a rapid blood sample from the carotid artery and sealed the needle puncture. She attached the sample end to a square device the size of her palm, with an LCD screen at the top and several buttons below the screen. While the sample was processed, Oracle began taking readings of the breath still in her nasal cavity, throat, and from the lungs with a long tube to reach in. After that was finished, she used other pieces to remove skin tissue samples from across the girl's entire body, clothing samples, hair samples.

Oracle's total time on the girl's body: one minute.

"What is her name?" she asked aloud.

From behind Spy's massive frame in the doorway a woman answered, "Jessica Matthews."

Oracle placed her glove over the girl's heart. "Rest in peace, Jessica. We will find who did this, and he will regret what he did to you…"

CHAPTER 12

CLUE

O h, God!!!" Dagen cried.

Amanda looked up from the magazine she was reading on the couch while her daughter was watching the television. "What?" she asked.

"Jessica's dead!" Dagen cried, pointing at the screen.

They both looked on in shock as the local television reporter detailed the death of Jessica in the middle school earlier in the day.

"What?" Amanda said again, leaning forward toward the TV. "What happened?"

Dagen didn't answer, only watching someone's phone camera video of a male figure and a long-black-haired woman, both dressed in form-fitting black uniforms, were guided into the school entrance. They listened in silence as the reporter commented only on that the girl was dead, but without the reason why, with "B-roll" footage of the reporter asking her fellow students earlier about what happened, how they knew Jessica, and so on, as was typical of any terrible event anywhere.

"It's crazy," Dagen whispered, tears flowing down her

cheeks. "It's, like, I just saw her yesterday and she was perfectly fine…"

"What were you doing yesterday with her?"

"Ran into her after school. We were both walking home and just met up at the same time a couple streets back."

"Anything strange happen?" Amanda asked. "Cough, sneeze, cough on you?"

"No. We just hugged like always, then started talking about our classes at our schools, clothes, stuff like that."

Amanda lifted her hand to Dagen's face to wipe the tears away. "It's okay, baby. Someone will figure out what happened. Let's just pray that whatever it was, was fast so that she didn't suffer…"

"Look at this, Agent Oracle," said the Task Force coroner.

Angela stepped forward and looked into the high-magnification microscope's eye lenses. She knew what she was supposed to see in a blood sample, so what she saw surprised her. "What the hell are those things?"

The coroner, Chris Andros, pressed a button on the microscope, sending a digital image of the microscope sample to a large wall screen. "Those black floaters? I have no idea what they are. Never seen anything like this before."

"Well, they certainly don't belong in anyone's blood," Angela answered. "Any idea what they do?"

"Nothing yet. It's like they just float there, that's all."

Angela crossed her arms. "We have permission from the Department of Health and Human Services to work this case as we see fit. We had her body rerouted to one of our forensic offices and is being routed here. Please begin an immediate autopsy when she arrives."

"Yes, ma'am," he replied.

"And remember," she added as she turned to leave, "her name is Jessica…"

Night had long since fallen, and Proteus was finishing her investigation of the classroom death scene, with Spy still guarding the door while police officers continued questioning school staff who were waiting their turns. "Status?" he asked.

Proteus turned her face to him, tapping her glasses wing to stop the data feed in her field of vision. "This is all so clean. Absolutely nothing I see is of value. Even the little info from Chris? Absolutely no trace anywhere."

He stood silently, contemplating. After a couple minutes he said, "So this is targeted. Pack up and let's get back to Division. You drive; I gave Oracle mine to go back earlier."

"You got it."

Spy turned to the female sergeant and said through his vocal enhancer, "This is a crime scene. No one in until you hear from me." He reached into a belt pouch next to his buckle and produced a business card; on it was a phone number. "This is the number I, or one of my team, will call you from with the okay."

She took it from him as he began to walk away, followed by the diminutive Proteus. "But you don't have my number?"

He stopped and turned back to her. "Don't I? " He continued walking toward the exit without another word.

After they were in her car and on the road, Proteus said, "You like doing that to people, don't you?"

He nodded, saying, "Shits and giggles, Pro. Shits and giggles…"

CHAPTER 13

ANOMALY

"Can you believe these deaths going on?" Marie said to Amanda.

"It's crazy," Amanda said to her fellow waitress. "Patti at the bank, the students…I just don't understand! Doesn't seem like there's any pattern to it!"

The young black co-worker said, "You're sounding like a cop now."

Amanda laughed. "Yeah, as if I had the brains for that kinda work. I'm happy where I am, thank you very much. Still…it just boggles the mind…"

"…boggles the mind," Angela sat in her father's office.

"Oh?" Mark asked, leaning back in his chair.

"An unknown contaminant in her blood," she answered. "Doesn't seem to do shit. She's otherwise healthy."

"Nothing more from Chris yet?"

"Only that he's pissed he can't figure it out."

Mark leaned forward, crossing his arms on his desktop. "You're more pissed that you can't, either."

She smiled. "You know me too well."

"Damn well do," he replied. "Taught you everything you know to be you."

"Well, then, you know I'm double-pissed inside. Can't find this Terrence, can't figure this thing in Jessica's blood. You're right, coincidences aren't to be believed."

"So," Mark announced, "we have a mystery terrorist and a mystery death. Two mysteries make a bigger mystery. But they don't necessarily have anything to do with each other; that's the other half of that coin." He saw her brow furrowed and her eyes staring at the wall. "What?"

"What if they are connected but are also a misdirection?"

"That's quite a reach."

"Time to leave the box, Daddy."

"I agree." He stood behind his desk. "But I assume you've already done your deepest matrix search on 'Mister Terrence'."

"What little there is to find. Aside from his name, it's like he's a spook."

"Ex-agent? Deep Undercover? Assassin for hire?"

"Yes…and no…and maybe."

"You're not helping, Angel."

"That's why you and the Navy are paying me these big bucks."

There came a knock from the open office pocket door. "Enter," said Mark.

Ensign Cutter entered the office, tablet in hand. "For you, Commander. Just got transmitted.

Angela took the offered device and read the message on the screen. "Um…we got something."

"Do share, Commander," Mark ordered for Cutter's benefit.

"There was another death recently. A bank teller passed

away at her till preparing for the day. Cause of death listed as 'unknown'." She saw Mark moving to get his gear. "How about I handle this, Dad—Captain."

He stopped moving, thought for a moment, then nodded his head silently.

Angela rose from her seat and handed the tablet back to Cutter. "Text me where she's currently being kept," she ordered the ensign.

"Aye, sir," Cutter responded.

Oracle brought her car to a stop in front of the morgue in eastern Centreville. Her car door automatically locked when she closed it, and she made her way to the front door, placing her federal badge on her uniform breast. Once inside she stepped to the receptionist's station. "I'm here to see Dr. Harris."

The receptionist, a young blond man in his mid-20s, replied, "Name?" When he saw the gun on her hip he said, "Are you police? That's not a uniform I'm familiar with."

"This is the only time I'll tell you to look at my breast," she said with a straight face. His eyes saw the federal badge and widened. "My apologies, agent!" He pressed the intercom. "Dr. Harris, federal agent to see you."

"Tell him 'Oracle'," she whispered.

"Agent Oracle."

A minute later a balding middle-aged man in a blue surgical suit came through the door leading into the offices and exam rooms. "Well, Agent Oracle, not like I expected you to look like that."

"I'm not exactly a day type," she said.

"Well, let's show you what I got…

"…and this is the only anomaly you found in your examination?" Oracle asked, her eyes focused on the microscope lenses.

"That's it. I mean, there's the proof of childbirth, residual alcohol from prior twelve hours, never a smoker, contusion from impacting the floor when she dropped…the usual stuff. But this? Beats the hell out of me what it is. But I can't confirm that this killed her."

"But you also can't deny it," she countered.

"No, I can't deny it. But it's just there, doing nothing!"

Oracle "hmphed" more to herself than to him.

Dr. Harris, however, recognized that tone. "You've seen it before, haven't you? Where?"

She rose and returned her black glasses to cover her eyes. "High school student across town. Exact same conditions, same anomaly in her blood, no other apparent cause of death."

"So, how'd you hear about this lady here?" Her quiet reply was her answer. "Yeah, 'need to know' stuff. Gotcha. So, what can I do to help?"

Oracle sat in his desk chair unbidden. "Honestly, I have no idea yet."

He sat in the chair on the outside of his desk. "I can tell it's beating the shit out of you, young lady."

"Am I that obvious?"

Harris smiled. "When you've seen enough dead people as I have, and as many people reacting to those people being dead, you learn how to read ALL physical reactions. And you've got a quite a mystery, don't you?"

Again, no reply.

"Is this something to be very concerned about? Another COVID? Or some other contagion that may be a mass killer?"

"Honestly, I have no idea. Two matching deaths doesn't

mean either of those possibilities.”

“Two mystery deaths,” he corrected.

“Granted. Not to make a gallows joke, but if there was a third matching death—”

“I believe you, Agent,” Harris said. “I don’t want to see it either, God forbid. But if you want these two deaths explained…”

Oracle’s phone in her belt beeped. She saw his eyebrows raise. “Don’t even think it.” She removed it from its belt pocket. “Why didn’t you just buzz my comm?” she asked tersely.

“Maybe because you don’t have it?” her father’s voice replied over the phone. “I’m holding it in my hand.”

“Oh,” she said. “So, what’ve you got?” She listened for a few seconds, then returned the phone to its pocket. Oracle looked into Harris’ eyes as she said, “Might be getting an explanation sooner than desired…”

CHAPTER 14

REMEMBER

A containment site had already been established on the Task Force Division grounds by the time Oracle arrived. Instead of parking in the garage, she brought her car to a stop beside the temporary building; her father was standing by the door. She asked as she exited her car, "What do we have here?"

He was wearing his mask, but his vocoder was turned off, allowing his normal voice to come through. "Teenage male, dropped dead during baseball practice. Because we already got involved in one, we've been asked to take over the entire case, with CDC answering to us."

"Pleasant change of pace," she said. "Hated being told when to and when not to wear a mask last time... So, what are the precautions?"

He handed her the ear comm she left behind; she took it and put it in her right ear. "Standard protection. Fortunately, our last uniform upgrades already provide that level already, just cover your head." He handed her a head mask similar to his, but it had a larger face screen opening.

"Says the guy already covered head to toe." She pulled it over her head, and he started patting it against her uniform on her back.

"Special adhesive sticks to the material for a full seal," Spy said. As he attached a small air tank to her belt and ran a hose from its nozzle to a plug in the back, he continued, "This will give you air for about two hours."

"Why don't you just get me a mask like yours?"

"Mine is trademarked," he chided.

"Ha, ha. So, lead the way."

The father and daughter agents entered through the door into a decontamination chamber. The door closed behind them; blasts of air hit them from all directions as fans sucked in everything blown off their uniforms. A stronger fan began blowing over the next door inward, with the opening glowing bright red, and its air containing special decontaminants. When it stopped blowing, the light turned bright blue and the door opened automatically.

They stepped into a massive medical complex, built to accommodate at least a dozen bodies, with full surgical sets in place for each bed. Four bodies were already laying at rest on their respective beds. "How hard was it to get the first victims here and all this assembled while I was out?"

"You have to ask?" Spy answered.

"Yeah, I should know better," Oracle added. "Orders, sir?"

"Commander, you have one order: solve this damn thing before we have another COVID situation."

She turned to face him at attention and saluted. "Aye, sir."

"And stay in constant communication with me on our private frequency. I don't care what you say, I want to hear it. Never know if you'll say something offhand that I need to know. Everyone here knows you're in command. Get it done."

"Will do." She stepped away to the first medical bay to talk with the physician in a Level A suit over the bank teller's still form.

Spy turned around to depart the building. After going through the second decontamination round he stepped outside and stopped at his daughter's car. "Hunter, Seeker, Proteus…report."

One at a time each replied, "Nothing."

Saying it aloud more than asking them, he replied, "What the hell is happening here?"

"Mom, what is happening here?" Dagen asked. "Now it's Gabe who's dead!!!"

Amanda hugged her daughter on the living room couch. "I don't understand either, little bug," she replied, holding her closer. "When did you see him last?"

"This morning after science class," she said between sniffs and tears. "Said he was placed to be starting pitcher for tonight's game against Fairfax. His first time starting! I gave him a kiss on the cheek for luck—"

"—that was sweet—"

"—but now he'll never get to be starting pitcher!" Dagen burst into screams and cried harder. "Who is doing this to my friends?"

Amanda cried with her. "I don't know, bug, I don't know…"

EARLIER THAT AFTERNOON…

"Good to see you again, Amanda."

Amanda suddenly felt her body shiver at the sound of that magnificent godlike English accent. Through a throat suddenly dry as a desert, she replied without looking around, "Mis-Mister Terrence?"

When she could finally turn she faced the man she was falling for deep inside. "Hello, madam," he said, taking off his bowler and bowing his head. "Been a bit since my last repast here; hope I haven't come before your shift end."

Her face was blushing deep red. "Oh, heavens, no…well, maybe getting close, but I can stay for you. Um…" she waved to a booth behind him "…is this okay?"

He looked toward the table, then turned and smiled at her. "It will suit perfectly." Terrence set his bowler on the table and sat on the far seat to continue viewing her. "Today I wish to order the steak, medium rare, loaded baked potato, house salad with Thousand Island dressing, and sweet iced tea, if I may, please."

Amanda felt like he was singing to him. "Um, yes, right away…I'll, um, be right back." She walked away gently so as not to pass out on the floor. At the waitress' station she held onto the edges to calm herself before punching the order into the terminal.

Another black waitress, Tabby, stepped up beside her and saw the badly flushed cheeks. "Girl, are you okay?" she asked, placing her hand on Amanda's forearm gently.

Amanda touched her hand back. "I'm ok, Tabby… I just…do you see that man in 27?"

Tabby looked up toward that table without being obvious. Her eyes widened. "Holy shit, babe, he's gorgeous!"

Amanda started blushing again. "Tell me about it!" she whispered. "Every time I hear his voice…or see him…it's like I'm waiting for him to sweep me off my feet!"

Tabby sucked in her breath. "Mandy! That is NO way to talk in public!" she said in an excited whisper. "But, oh, man, I could feel the same way…"

"I'm gonna punch in his order and go to the bathroom and calm myself…"

"I hear ya, girl… Mm, mm, he is a hottie!"

"Commander," one of the Task Force medics said to Oracle, "The next ambulance is arriving from the transfer center."

"Guide him to Bay 2, straight to Bed 6 and alert Team 6 to meet me there."

"Aye, sir," he said, saluted, and left to follow her orders.

She took off her uniform glasses and pinched the bridge of her nose. *How the hell am I supposed to stop a potential epidemic if I don't know what I'm looking for?* She put her dark glasses back on and headed for Bed 6 inside. *First step is to see if this victim's blood has this same strange whatever it is as the other five...*

In her spare time over the years as permanent liaison assigned by Naval Intelligence to the Task Force Division, Angela studied and earned a medical degree, giving her the ability to not only oversee this secure operation but also participate in the medical research...including this multi-victim event. "Garibaldi," she said to the nurse in her Level A suit, "blood sample before anything. Get it on a slide and put it on the screen."

"Aye, sir," she responded, and went straight to work.

"Hutchins," Oracle said to the driver, also in HazMat, along with the rest of the teams. "Short version."

"Nothing unusual," he replied, "just driving home from work. Witness reported seeing her suddenly slump over in her seat, and then her car went through a barrier, crashed in a gulley by the highway. TF agents are on scene, securing the area and preparing her vehicle for transport here."

"Bernard, Oracle."

"I read you," she heard his assistant reply.

"Contact Victim 6 first responders, tell them to stand down. Code 3."

"Code 3, aye, sir."

The failure to resolve the crisis notwithstanding, Oracle

kept her stead by coordinating the people around her as her mind played through logical scenario after scenario. When Garibaldi said, "Ready, sir," she cleared her thoughts and moved to get a view of the large plasma screen above the foot of the victim's bed. "Let's see it," Oracle ordered.

The screen flared to life and immediately played an image of the victim's blood sample: red corpuscles, white corpuscles…and those same strange little dots of mystery as in the other victim.

Oracle began to fume…

Six years ago, following the Black Widow affair, her father evaluated her performance in the hotel stairwells to catch the murderess before finally confronting her in the large public room. "You acted appropriately, if impetuously," he said. "Your mind was in the right spot, but your logic was not."

"I don't understand, Daddy," she replied.

"You rushed to judgement, to get into the field, which was not your job in this mission."

"But no one was responding to my hails."

"Irrelevant. You should have found a way. The communications department has many ways to reach any of us, even on silent running."

"There was no ti—"

"Did you read the Division manual?"

"Every page, Daddy."

"Section 4, Chapter 3."

Angela's eyes narrowed as she reread the text in her eidetic memory. "Oh, shit."

"Yes, ma'am, shit," he said. "You so wanted to come be part of capturing a serial killer that you broke protocol…not that you didn't have the authority, just not in this case."

"I—I—you're right, Daddy…sir."

"You're not going to be reprimanded or anything like that, however."

"But I should be!"

"Commanding officer's discretion. I'm going to send you off for some special training."

"But I'm only just getting my department staffed my way, getting the training going right—"

Mark stopped her with the palm of his hand in the air. "Not today, Angel. You finish building your department, but no more field jaunts. Not until after you see Ho Choy."

Her eyes widened. "You're sending me to learn under your master???"

"Yup. But he's not going to teach you to fight. I've asked him to prepare a series of lessons on expanding your spatial acuity." He rose from his desk to sit beside her in the second chair in front of his desk. "You have a one in a billion mind. But Choy…it's like he's an immortal. With a sentence he can show you the universe. A word, the world beneath your feet. But what he can do for you—" he lightly pressed a finger on her forehead "—is free the limitations of even your advanced analytics."

"Will he teach me…your secrets?"

Mark smiled wide and hugged his daughter tightly. "I didn't tell him 'no'…nor did I tell him 'yes'. He'll decide if you're ready for those particular… talents…"

She closed her eyes and concentrated within herself as she had learned years earlier. *"Ignore the chaos, as it is always there. Search for the chaos that is out of place."* "Magnification 5K," Oracle ordered. The technician at the electron microscope complied. The screen shifted with a horizontal wipe to show the same view a thousand times larger. Oracle stepped closer to the screen to concentrate on the image as best she could through her secure head cover. "What's that?" she said aloud several minutes later.

"What's what, sir?" he asked.

"Overlay grid," she ordered. Moments later a series of horizontal and vertical lines appeared on the screen. "Shift grid to red." The lines changed from orange to red in color. "Increase density 500% and number." Five times as many lines appeared on screen, which each square of image including a number. She stared intently at the various numbered images created by the intersecting lines. Several minutes passed in silence as she examined every square, until she said, "Grid 167, isolate and fill the screen."

The technician recalibrated his computer view until that one microscopic view filled the screen.

Garibaldi said it first. "Mother fu—"

Oracle nodded. "Mother, indeed." She looked down on the victim in the bed from the foot end. "Who is this victim who provided us our first clue?"

Garibaldi looked at her tablet. "Tabitha Gaines. Worked as a waitress. Preferred to go by her nickname, Tabby…"

CHAPTER 15

INITIAL

The Task Force Field Team, plus Division Director Tom Michelson, gathered in the conference room off the Field Team offices hallway.

After they were all settled, Mark called the meeting to order. Like the other members, he was still dressed in his uniform, though the front was zipped down a few inches and he did not wear his full hood nor gloves. The other members were similar, sitting without their computer glasses or gloves on. "I know we're tired," he started. "And it seemed like we were chasing our asses like we were dogs, not knowing why we were going in circles, but that's all we seemed to be able to do. Thanks to Angela, we finally have one answer."

Angela rose from her seat and went to the front viewscreen, which flared to life when she pressed the remote control in her hand. Last night our sixth victim of mysterious death arrived here. I concentrated first on a blood sample, as the other victims turned out to have this same anomaly in their blood." She clicked the remote five times, taking her time between each. "These images are at highest possible magnification with current technology, 1000 times.”

Harri said, “They look like little balls…marbles, even. There’s nothing descript on any screen.”

“Correct,” Angela said. “The first five victims got here hours, even a few days after they passed. That’s what we got from all of them after we had a chance to examine number 5. However, we got number 6 within approximately 40 minutes of her passing.”

“How were we notified?” Mae-Lei asked.

“I ordered any death of mysterious cause to be sent to our offsite facility for ‘autopsy’, which brought them here to our emergency center outside,” Mark replied. “Broke a lot of speed limits getting it here. Be sure to pay any fines the cameras caught, Tom.”

“Take it up with the Secretary,” Tom said, laughing.

“So, what did number 6 provide?” Calvin inquired to get the meeting back on track.” Angela looked at Calvin as she brought up the next image. He started to rise to his feet. “What the hell is that? I mean, are those?”

“What are they exactly? I don’t know yet. But applying some long reach logic, I think this is the delivery system of what killed these people.”

On the screen was a blood sample, similar to the others she displayed, but on this final one the dark little orbs all had small medical-needle-type projections across their surfaces.

“To make this even more interesting, this next image is the exact same sample, not even removed from the microscope.”

The next image showed all the same dark little orbs, now smooth as marbles.

Angela sat in her seat at the end of the table, beside where her father sat at the head. “Based on before and after images, I’d have to deduce that these little orbs are the delivery system for whatever this plague or virus or whatever it is.”

“Is this man-made?” Mae asked.

“Based on my studies so far, absolutely. Those little orbs…they are just too perfect. Now, I’m speculating, but with applied logic: these orbs are delivered somehow, then are on a delay before dispensing whatever drug or whatever it is into the victim, then going into dormant mode again so that if ever seen in a microscope well after the deceased is examined all it looks like is dirtballs in the blood stream."

Harri asked, "Is it possible to slice open one of those microscopic meatballs to see how they work?"

Angela smiled. "I thought you'd never ask."

Mark said, "Harri, you're with Angela…AFTER you both get some rest. Angela, make sure the medical suite contacts ME with any updates, I'll wake you if warranted. Bernard, you get them whatever they need. Calvin, Mae, get some rest. This is the clue we needed to get started, but it's a very, very, tiny clue. Dismissed."

The agents left for their duties, leaving Mark, Tom, and Cutter in the conference room. "That ain't much to go on, Mark," said Tom.

"Minute as it is, at least it's something," Mark countered.

Tom took a deep breath before saying, "Carl Sagan said, '…the total number of stars in the universe is greater than all the grains of sand on all the beaches of the planet Earth.' Doubt he ever considered cells in the bloodstream."

"He likely did. Only his mind could consider that quantifiable calculation, though." He turned his attention to his assistant. "Cutter, send a message, please."

"Yes, sir?" she replied.

"Send on satellite frequency TF13: 'Tā zhǔnbèihǎo le'."

"Sir?"

Mark smiled. "Sorry. I'll write it down for you…"

◆

An hour later, an elderly man was in his modest little house on the western side of Beijing, sitting in quiet contemplation with a cup of Oolong tea, when a small light in a flowerpot on his table slowly flashed. He stepped to the table, sat in the only chair, and opened the side of the pot to reveal a small speaker with several buttons along the left side. "Shuō," he said softly.

"Tā zhǔnbèihǎo le'," said a female voice.

He closed the side of the flowerpot and returned to his tea, a big smile slowly spread across his face…

CHAPTER 16

AWAKE

Angela Jason hated when someone else is right…except for her father. The short, but deep, sleep was more energizing than she would admit to anyone, but she was in a far better attitude when she returned to her office.

"Good morning, Commander," said Ensign Bernard. "You're looking very rested."

"I hate to say, Ensign…but you're correct. I feel much better. Any updates?"

"No, sir," he said.

She smiled. "Would you be so kind as to bring some coffee to the captain's office? One for you and me, please."

Her polite attitude after her recent contained anger caught him off guard, if only momentarily. "My pleasure, sir."

"Thank you." Angela continued on to her father's office. She knocked gently. On the wall by the open doorway.

"Enter."

"Good morning, Daddy," she said with a smile. She sat across from him at his desk.

Mark moved his hands away from his computer keyboard. "Well, now, you look more like the daughter of Jan Jason this morning."

"Mark Jason, too," she said. Bernard entered with two cups of coffee, handing one to Angela. "I'll say it once, and we'll move on: you're right, I needed the sleep, and let's get back on case. Got any updates?"

Mark smiled just slightly before complying. "A couple more victims during the night. Following your discovery, both were given blood tests as soon as we received them. Exact same nodules in the bloodstreams, same extended points, and after what we calculate to be an hour after releasing whatever they released into the blood the points retracted, and whatever killed the victims seemingly dissipated." Mark sipped at his own coffee. "I'll save you the speech Tom gave me; Centreville is starting to panic, the National Guard is on standby, the CDC is preparing to extend a quarantine, and the call I got from The President is not one I wanted, not that he understood all the technobabble I gave him. He's not doing a national address yet." He leaned forward on his desk. "Angela, I love you, and you are amongst the smartest people on this planet. I need answers…NOW."

"Aye, sir," she said. She calmly sat back in her chair and held her coffee cup in both hands. "We have, what now, eight or nine victims?"

"Bernard?" said Mark. "I've been too busy to keep count.

"Nine total, sirs," the ensign answered.

"That's a good number to start with," she said, almost under her breath.

"Come again?" Mark asked.

She gently sipped her coffee again. "Bernard, I need a geographical map on the conference room screen. Plot the locations of all the victim's discovery locations. We'll meet you there."

"Aye, sir," he said, doing an about-face and leaving the office.

"You have a plan?" Mark asked.

"I have a rested mind, Captain," she said. "And…maybe an idea."

"This is right now an exercise in logical assumption," Angela said to the Field Team in the main conference room. She extended her pointer to several red dots on the map. "Ensign Bernard plotted all the victims' discovery locations on this map of Centreville." She stood back to allow everyone to see the large screen easily.

"What does it tell you?" Mae asked.

Setting her pointer on the table as she sat in her seat, she said, "Not a damn thing."

"Frustration rising again, Commander?" Mark said pointedly.

"No, sir," she confessed. "Daddy—Captain, team members, I am great with information gathering, plotting, and such. But not in deductive reasoning, I'm sorry."

Harri reached out and put her arm around Angela's shoulders. "Hey, girlfriend, not to worry. You've done your part to date. We're here to help do the rest."

Angela looked at her father, her eyes questioning. She watched as her father's stern look…the look of a commander and a killer, if necessary…soften into a small grin, and his eyes' terrifying squint softened and the crow's feet at his eyes' corners became pronounced. "My congratulations, Angela."

"But, what?"

Mark said, "You've got the fourth highest IQ on this planet. Everything you've ever done intellectually you've succeeded. But as Captain Kirk might have said in 'Star Trek', this was your 'Kobayashi Maru Scenario'. You never would have been stressed in a simulation; you would have figured it out immediately. So even though this is an actual major crisis, this was a perfect time to test your reactions as the leader in this investigation. And you passed with high marks."

The team members applauded.

Angela looked at them, then back at her father. "Lousy ass time to test me." That elicited chuckles from the others. "However, it was logically the perfect time to do so."

"My daughter, Mister Spock's sister!"

Harri said, "Remember, no one's supposed to remember her!"

Calvin said, "Quoth the team geek!"

Everyone began laughing for several seconds before Mark brought them back to reality. "Okay, all, we've had some relaxation. Let's turn on the brains."

Mae rose from her seat and walked to the screen at the front of the room. "Ensign Bernard," she said to Angela's assistant.

"Sir?"

"Can you add the victims' information next to each plot point?"

"Aye, sir." He tapped on his laptop at the far end of the conference table. "All added, sir."

Mae looked at the information blocks that appeared on the screens. "Names, addresses, sexes…how about the ages?"

"Some of that was redacted from official records due to their ages," he replied.

Mae swung her head around to him. "What about their ages?"

"All but two are minors…"

CHAPTER 17

UNCONNECTED

I don't give a rat's ass about 'age', show me the numbers," Angela ordered.

"Aye, sir, running decryption." Only a minute later the spot points on the screen included the victims' ages.

"They're all high school age," Harri remarked.

"They are, indeed," Angela agreed. She looked at her father, his return gaze unreadable. "So why are all but two so young?"

"How many high schools are involved?" Mark said.

Bernard answered, "Four, sir."

"No even distribution of victims," Calvin noted.

Mark looked at Angela again. "So, let's concentrate on the school with the most victims," she said.

"What about the adult victims?" Mark asked.

"Damn," Angela replied. "How DO they fit into this? Otherwise, this looks like a teenager serial killer."

Bernard said, "The first adult victim was a bank teller, the second a restaurant waitress."

Harri rose and walked to the screen. "Their locations are

fairly close to each other," she said, pointing at their spots on the screen. "Coincidence?"

"Nothing at this point would indicate yes or no," Angela said. "But, it is a good question. Were they both killed at their jobs?"

"The teller was; the waitress was at home."

"Bernard, where is the waitress' job location?"

"One moment, Commander," he said. A few button-presses later a new location icon appeared on the screen, even further away.

"Not logical," Angela said under her breath.

Mark offered, "Perhaps the death location is an accidental misdirection; maybe she was infected at work."

"That would have the restaurant and bank in closer proximity if so," Angela agreed. "But, since the bulk are teen victims, are the two adults accidental…or the source."

Mark stood. "Angela, those are questions you take outside to our coroners. Mae, Harri, go to the bank and the restaurant, standard follow-ups. Calvin, you're with me. Dismissed."

The team members left the conference room, Bernard closed his computer and left the room as well, leaving only Mark and Calvin in the room. "We doing the schools?" Calvin asked.

"Nope," Mark said.

"Why not?"

"The emotional trauma is still high there, with all the involved schools, even non-involved schools, having additional counselors on hand to help the living students deal with the trauma. Our interference would only make it worse."

"Makes sense. So, what ARE we going to do?"

"The most difficult thing…wait…keep researching…"

"Patti Key was absolutely the first," the head coroner told

Angela, who tapped that information into her tablet. "That nodule system we found in her blood was easy to date as the oldest."

"How so?"

"It's definitely man-made," he said, pointing at the screen above her body in the cool environment. "Remember when you saw it the first time? That's the image on the left. On the right is a sample we took an hour ago…it's lost its near-perfect symmetry, and now looks like a bad golf ball. It's heavily pitted, parts of the surface look like they've broken off…"

"How long until it's totally dissipated from her body?"

"At this rate, perhaps another day."

Her table automatically updated everything from Patti's bio monitors. "And the last victim?"

"Tabby, yes. The latest blood slide shows her nodules are only perfect little spheres, the points have either broken off or withdrawn or dissipated themselves, we missed the opportunity to witness that particular action."

She looked at the new data loading to her tablet. "Looks like about an hour between when those points appear and disappear." She took a deep breath. "I hate to say it, but we need another victim…"

CHAPTER 18

BISHOP

Mister Terrence pressed a single number on his phone. "Report," said the familiar soft German-accented voice.

"Position Bishop," Terrence said.

"Details."

"By this point in time the special mechanism should have been found in one of the targets' blood."

"Any media coverage?"

"Only that there were some mysterious deaths in area high schools, counselors have been brought into those schools."

The German voice was silent for several seconds. "But nothing on the mysterious agents?"

Terrence sighed. "No, sir."

"Unfortunate," said the voice. "All these years developing the perfect means of 'hooking them', as the Americans say, and nothing."

"Sir, if I may?"

"Speak clearly," the German voice said, irritation obvious and the threat unmistakable.

"The agents may already be on the case."

"Indeed? And just how do you arrive at that assumption?"

"Simple, sir…because there is no word about investigations underway means precisely that there are indeed investigations underway."

The German voice was silent for many seconds. "Logical," he finally said. "Yes, the lack of its existence is confirmation that it exists. Very good, Mister Terrence."

"Thank you, sir."

"Bishop to Queen 2," said the voice, and the call disconnected.

Mister Terrence returned his phone to his vest pocket and began contemplating the next step…

CHAPTER 19

INQUIRY

Amanda was surprised by the appearance of the petite woman who entered the restaurant: dressed in skin-tight black with a gun on her hip, badge on her chest, and narrow dark glasses. Still rattled by Tabby's sudden death, she approached her professionally. "Would you like a table?" she asked the apparent cop or fed.

"I'd like to speak with your manager, please," the woman countered.

"She's not in, right now; I'm the head waitress, if I can help."

"Got time to sit and talk with me?"

Amanda stuttered for a moment. "I-I'm really not allowed—"

"I understand," she interrupted. "Still, since I'm here, just a minute of your time."

Amanda remembered the rules of her hiring, but all the recent deaths of students made her decide to the contrary, especially if it would help protect Dagen. "It's slow, we can sit here for a moment." She motioned at the booth they stood beside, and they both took opposite seats from each other. "Only until my manager returns."

"Understood. I am Agent Proteus, Federal Investigator."

"Odd name."

"You've no idea," Proteus said with a smile. "You're aware of all the student deaths lately."

"You've no idea," Amanda returned, also smiling. "My daughter is the same age as all these other students, and she keeps me up to date on all the class chattering."

"Noted. Are you aware of the two adults—"

"Yes," Amanda replied. "I knew them both."

Proteus raised an eyebrow. "Indeed? When was the last time you saw them both?"

"Well, Tabby works with me—I mean, 'worked'—the day before she passed. And Patti, at the bank, I saw her when I deposited my cash tips for the day."

"Aren't you supposed to report your cash tips?"

"Oh, I do! I pay my taxes properly—"

Proteus raised her gloved hand. "No worries, I don't work in the Treasury Department. I'm here to investigate these deaths. You were saying?"

"Oh, yes…I saw Patti when I deposited my cash—"

"How long later did you learn she died?"

"The next morning, on the news when I was getting ready for work."

"Did Patti Key look ill, or flushed, or anything unusual?"

Amanda though for several seconds, trying to recall her deposit visit. "No, she looked perfect as usual."

Proteus pulled a business card from a pocket on her belt. The only thing on that card was a phone number. "If you think of anything else, this is my direct number. Call it."

"I will, thank you."

Shifting the conversation, Proteus asked, "You said you have a daughter? How's she handling all this?"

"She's badly upset and scared."

"Understandable. Did she know any of the students?"

Amanda began to answer, but her open mouth froze for several sections. "Um…as a matter of fact, she knew all of them."

"Interesting," Proteus said, matter-of-factly. "Do you suppose I could speak with her? With your permission and presence, of course."

"I—I guess that would be okay, if you keep it short…and don't upset her. First time she gets upset again I will ask you to leave."

"Absolutely. And thank you for your permission in advance. What time do you get home?"

"Today…I get off at 4, get home around 4:15 or so."

Proteus rose from the booth. "I'll meet you at your apartment at 4:30." She turned to leave.

"But—but, I haven't given you my address."

The agent turned around and smiled. "I'll see you at 4:30." She walked to the restaurant entrance and opened the door to leave, just as the manager was entering. Amanda quickly yanked the towel from her waist and began wiping the table.

Her manager, Karen Battle, stopped at her table. "Taking a break, are we?" she asked Karen, politely but indicating there might be an infraction.

"No, ma'am, just cleaning the table from the last user."

Karen nodded her head, "Okay, no problem…not like we've got a busy house between meals." She offered her hand to help Amanda get out of the booth.

She took Karen's hand in hers and slid out of the booth and to her feet.

"Finish your shift and go home. The evening crew has checked in, and there are no reservations. I'm sure Dagen could use you right now."

"Thank you, Miss Battle."

Her manager smiled. "Never a problem. Family comes first. Get outta here."

As Karen continued to her office, Amanda smiled to

herself as she finished her work with the tables and evening crew.

▼ ▼ ▼

"Good evening," Proteus said as she was allowed to enter the apartment. First thing she noticed was the teenage girl sitting on the couch, completely covered in a huge comforter except for her head.

"Dagen, sweetheart, this is Agent Proteus. She'd like to talk with you about your friends—"

"Only if you're up to it," Proteus interrupted. "If not, I'll leave and let you rest."

Dagen was unmoving, her tears streaked with drying tears.

After a few minutes of silence in the room, Proteus said, "I understand. You're grieving, I'd be just like you in a time like this. Your mom has my number; you can call me anytime you feel you could talk."

The petite agent rose, and a light reflected off her gun belt buckle into Dagen's eyes. Dagen blinked hard, and asked, "What is that?"

"What is what?" Proteus asked back.

"That design." Dagen pointed at the buckle.

"Oh. That's my agent symbol."

"What's it mean?"

"Well," Proteus said as she sat back down, "It represents my best talent."

"Triangles? Pyramids? I don't understand."

"It's ok…nothing to worry about. So…may I ask how you're doing?"

"I'm terrible. My friends…what's happening to my friends? Why are they dying? I don't want to go back to school…ever again…"

"We're working on that," Proteus replied. "It's a challenge to find out what's happening. But I'd like to know from you if any of them looked like they were sick or not their best."

"No," Dagen said, tears beginning to well in her eyes again, "every single one was in their peak of health, near as I could tell."

"And you? Aside from your heart breaking, and I truly sympathize, how do you feel? Ill? Sick? Tummy ache, or—"

"No, I'm fine…I'm…" She started to sob.

"It's ok, you can let it out. Best thing you can do." She rose and stepped to Amanda, who had been watching their exchange from several feet away.

"Did you get what you wanted?" Amanda asked.

"Yes, and no," Proteus said. "She's in a lot of emotional pain; you may want to consider taking her to a counsellor or psychiatrist. But for now, just be what you are right now…the best mother in the world."

Amanda smiled as she nodded her head, a tear of her own rolling down one cheek. "Thank you…I'm doing the best I can with all this. Are you sure you don't have any answers?"

"We've got a lot of questions, believe me. The answers…are proving to be quite challenging. The best minds in the country are working on this mystery, and I promise you when we find out what we are dealing with and who did it…there will be justice." She stepped back to Dagen and knelt before her wrapped-up figure. "You rest. Remember all the good things about your friends…those are the memories to celebrate now and for all the rest of your life. As long as you remember them, they'll never really be gone."

Dagen smiled. "Star Trek II: The Wrath of Khan."

This time Proteus smiled. "A fellow geek. I'm so glad to know you!" She rose again, this time to leave. On her way she reminded Amanda, "Call me, any time you think of anything that could help."

"Thank you for everything you're doing."

Proteus nodded, and as she opened the door she replied, "Thank us when we solve this mystery…"

The next morning, as Amanda was checking the morning news on her tablet, she read that her manager, Karen Battle, was found dead by her husband at their home…

CHAPTER 20

SCHOOLING

THE PRIOR DAY

gent Hunter, I'm Principal Kendal," the tall man said to the Hawaiian agent. "Pleased to meet you."

"Thank you for your time," Hunter said.

"Interesting uniform," he noted. "Which department do you belong to?"

"A special Federal investigative unit," she replied.

He motioned her to join him in his office, closing the door behind them to keep their conversation private. "Doesn't take a lot of guessing to realize, then, that you're investigating the student deaths."

"Correct. What can you tell me about the students who died?"

They sat at the same time. He said, "Completely mystified. They were all healthy, doing what they do during classes and after classes. No indication of illness or trauma from any single one. All the student and staff who saw them reported not a thing wrong with any of them…yet, here we are now, with—". He looked at a news bulletin on his desktop computer "—eleven students as of a minute ago. What the hell is going on, Agent? Are our students under some kind of directed attack? District hasn't even given the order to close the schools—"

"Excellent questions," said Hunter. "And no answers."

"No answers at all, or no answers you can provide?"

Hunter smiled. He couldn't see her eyes for the gl3asses but could read her body language easily enough. "Actually, both."

"I'd laugh if this wasn't such a serious matter. My kids here are scared, Agent Hunter. Nobody knows if they won't be coming back to school in the morning. The counsellors are doing—"

"I understand all the protocols you're following, and you're doing an excellent job. I can only say that what we're dealing with here is something we have never seen before, can't even describe it."

"Is this another COVID-19? Or Anthrax?"

"Nothing like that," she replied. "What we're dealing with isn't acting like a mass exposure. It's not following any pattern at all. And it's only in this area of the city. No cases have been found outside Centreville."

"Bizarre," he said.

"Good word for it." She handed him a card from a belt pouch. "This is my direct number. If you think of anything, notice anything out of the sort, please call me immediately."

"Of course."

Hunter rose. "Would you mind if I walked the campus? Just want to check it out for myself. And keep the kids in their classes while I do."

"I'll send notification to all teachers. Take as long as you need."

"Thank you, Principal Kendal. We hope to end this crisis as soon as possible."

"Thank you, Agent," he said as she opened his office door and left.

Hunter walked the halls at a leisurely pace, examining

every wall, locker door, classroom door, window, and so on. She said aloud softly, "Tactical, Hunter. Are you getting everything?"

"Hunter, Tactical," she heard in her ear comm. "All scans are coming in clear and are in immediate examination. Searching for any indication of the nodule."

"I'll just keep going, let me know if anything is triggered."

"Roger. Tactical going silent." The sound in her ear faded.

Hunter continued walking the hallways, finding nothing out of the ordinary. Her mind began drifting to her time at St. Anthony's Catholic School in her home state but snapped herself back to the present when a red light flashed in the top right of her lens. "Got an alert, Tactical. Read and advise."

She heard her tactical support's line as quiet but active in the background. Moments later her support voice said, "Nothing in the target. Just some marijuana."

Hunter smiled. "File the report to the principal for his discretion." She continued through every hall until she returned to the front office and the school entrance. "Spy, Hunter," she said aloud softly.

"Hunter, Spy," she heard in her ear. "Report."

"This school is clean, aside from one student harboring some weed."

"Very good…or bad, depending on how we look at this. School's about to let out for the day, return to base."

"Roger. Hunter out." She walked out the front entrance to her waiting department car. Once behind the wheel, she started the engine and drove out of the parking lot, heading for Task Force Division headquarters…

CHAPTER 21

SHARING

Well, naturally the girl knew all the teen victims," Mark said. "The way the schools interact for sports competitions and such and seeing each other after classes and on weekends and on and on…I think I'd be more concerned that she may be a future victim at most."

"And the mother?" Harri asked. "That she knew both the adult victims personally?"

Mark leaned forward on the conference table. "That…that is a bit more problematic. How was the mother…Amanda, is it?...how did she seem to you?"

"Professional when I spoke with her at the restaurant, and obviously more concerned about her daughter at home."

"The teen population at the school is obviously rattled," Mae added. "But nothing I could detect that indicated an infection source."

Mark sat back in his chair at the head of the conference table, rapping his knuckles on the surface. Angela entered the conference room at that moment. "Anything?" Mark asked her directly.

Angela sat in the chair nearest her father. "Another victim was just delivered. Was witnessed dying twenty minutes ago, doctors are doing live monitor of multiple blood samples."

Mark frowned in frustration. "Not good enough, people. No, I'm not mad or snapping at you…It's just the situation. Too many victims, not enough answers, no idea where to go next. Very frustrating."

Calvin was sitting on Mark's other side, across from Angela. "We're all in agreement with that," he offered.

Angela's phone vibrated in her belt's pouch. She withdrew it and answered the call on speaker mode. "Oracle."

"Agent," said Coroner Michael Brandon in the medical building, "we caught it!"

"Transmit to the conference room screen, please."

She and the team looked at the LCD screen at the far end of the room. It was a closeup view of the latest victim's blood, showing the mysterious round brown nodules floating with the red and white blood cells, but also with the little needle tip extensions still visible. A minute later they watched as the tips simply dissolved and disappeared into the blood plasma. "That was three minutes ago," Michael reported.

"Know where those particles went?"

"Far as we can determine right now, they dissolved to the atomic level. Never seen anything like this before."

"Thanks for that little bit," Angela said as she hung up. "Well, that was interesting."

"Just one more piece of an unknown puzzle," Mark said.

"I'm fully confident that this is a man-made…whatever it is. And it's designed to fall apart after releasing whatever it is that kills people."

"But…why?"

Calvin piped up first. "Obviously to get our attention."

"Definitely did that," said Harri.

"Was it intended to get our attention?" Mark queried.

"Well," his daughter replied, "intended or not, it did."

"Indeed, it did," Mark said. He looked toward Angela, but actually at the wall behind her, lost in his own thoughts.

"He's doing it again," Harri whispered to Angela, who quietly nodded in reply.

Mark concentrated deep within, organizing all the disparate pieces of evidence and information in his mind, with the team sitting in silence. After a few minutes he said aloud, "Is there anyone we've pissed off recently who escaped our grasp?"

"Like Talon?" Calvin said. "He's living in shadow world again, no known contact or sighting of him since he escaped during the Black Widow capture. It's been years…last I heard through my network was that he was back in Buenos Aires, but no one's been able to confirm that."

"That guy who called himself The Invisible Man," Harri offered, "couple years back swore after being found guilty and taken to prison that he'd get back at us for capturing him."

"And The Skull," Mae added. "Four years ago, we stopped him from bombing the White House. But I know he's still in jail, along with his gang."

"It's true we've had a number of, dare I say it, 'arch-villains' confront us. Either as a team or individuals. But they're all imprisoned, dead, or missing. Who among them have the knowledge to assemble this kind of killer virus? And how is it transmitted? And who is transmitting it?"

"Team 7 was studying the genetic makeup of the nodules from the last prior victim. Usually, such killers leave a signature of some kind, microscopically, as a way of showing 'I got you and you can't catch me'. They have yet to find such a marker." Angela interlaced her fingers on the tabletop and hung her head down partially.

"What a pain in the ass," Calvin said. "We've got the best organization in the world in this building, and we're stumped!"

"Angela," Mark added, "you said there was no microscopic signature…what about elemental markers?"

She lifted her head to look at him, her brow furrowed.

"No matter where a man-made virus was designed and created, it's got to contain atmospheric traces in the makeup, correct? Environmental evidence like how much percentage of breathable gasses are in the area?" He let the idea sink in for a few seconds. "Even the cleanest clean rooms for scientists are still going to contain exhales of technicians entering from the outside, despite the 'clean' protocols. Their breaths will contain traces of the external atmosphere. And even if not their breaths, the clothing will carry traces in fabric folds like in boot tucks and hoods, despite the sterilization processes…"

"So, we take the nodules apart to see what made them tick."

"Do it," Mark ordered. Without another word, Angela rose and departed the room.

Mae chuckled. "You're good, boss. A class act."

"How long do you think she'll take?" Harri asked.

Mark rose to his feet, also intending to leave the room. "I'll give her…an hour…to catch up to me…"

As the door closed behind him, the rest of the team sat with their mouths open in sudden shock…

CHAPTER 22

GUILT

TWO DAYS LATER

Two days had passed since the agent calling herself "Proteus" had visited them, and two more deaths of Dagen's friends. She refused to leave the apartment for any reason, not wanting to know if the next friend she saw would also be the last time.

Amanda took time off work to be with her daughter, holding her or sitting close by, depending on Dagen's mood. Amanda cried every time her daughter did, with absolutely no idea on how to even start being of help.

Dagen wanted the apartment as dark as possible; she didn't want to see out, didn't want light to come in. She turned her phone and tablet off, cutting herself off from everyone…and from any source of more possible bad news.

"I'm here for you," Amanda would often whisper to Dagen. "We'll get through this, my beautiful little bug."

All Dagen would do is give a quick smile, then bury herself deep into her comforter and blanket.

Who's doing this to us? Amanda thought to herself. *And why?…*

◆

"Yes, Mister President, our staff is on it 24/7… No, sir, we do not believe we're looking at another COVID event… Yes, sir, we are gathering many new leads…Solution, sir? As soon as humanly possible, yes, sir…Will do, sir." Tom Michelson set his desk phone in its cradle and looked at Mark, sitting across from his desk. "Okay, Spy, just how the hell much did I just lie to the President of The United States?"

Mark tilted his head in a "are you kidding me?" motion. "The day you tell me every elected official in this country is priestly is the day I tell you to stop lying to them," he replied. "But, the truth is the team is developing leads, despite their miniscule size."

"Well, give me something, dammit, so I can at least tell the White House we have a strong lead for a change."

"I'm waiting on an update from Oracle, actually…"

Corpsman John Harrison, working at one of the electronic microscopes, "Oh, holy, shit…"

"Speak up, Corpsman," Angela said from across the lab in the medical building next door to the administration building when she heard his exclamation. She dropped what she was studying at that exam table and walked to stand behind his chair.

"Sir," he said, "apologies for my outburst."

"No apologies," she said. "Just report what you have."

"Sir, your order was to examine and re-examine every piece of evidence we have—"

"Do I look like I want a recitation of my orders, Corpsman?"

"No, sir…but it does bear in, with your permission."

"Go," she said.

"Once we determined the life span of the nodules, I began looking at them for degradation times and characteristics…but then I noticed patterns. There are patterns in nature, yes, but not usually so in cellular-level forms."

"Are you saying you found designed characteristics in the nodules?"

"More than that, sir… I found Morse Code."

That made Angela's eyebrows rise, and her eyes open wide. "Morse Code…at the cellular level? Have you determined what it says?"

"By the time I got to the sixth victim's nodule evidence I finally figured it through. Look here, sir." Harrison pointed at his monitor when he brought up Patti's blood sample. "Here. These nodules are all degrading at the same pace but leaving the same configuration on their surfaces: three blue dots each."

"Three dots…that's an 'S'."

"Yes, sir. Here's victim 2."

She saw those nodules all with one blue dot on each. "One dot…an 'E'." Harrison then showed the third sample plate. "One dot again." The fourth plate's nodules had a blue dash/blue dot/blue dash combination on each. "A 'K'." She stood back. "Don't tell me the next one is also one dot, and the sixth one is a dot/dash/dot." Without saying a word, Harrison brought those evidence plates to the screen, with both plates' nodules with one having just one blue dot and the other the blue dot/dash/dot combination. "That spells 'Seeker'."

"Yes, sir."

"Son of a bitch…"

◆

IN THE CONFERENCE ROOM

"Me?" Calvin said in surprise.

"I've got to say it confirms our theory that this was all to get our attention," Mark said. "And you must be the target in this grand scheme."

"But who?" Angela said.

"Don't bother asking if I have any idea who would be up to something like this. The list is over twenty years old, just as a Task Force agent, never mind the military years," interjected Calvin.

"Do any of the later victims, number 7 and up, have any such markers on their degrading nodules?" Mark asked Angela.

"The ones that have reached this level of degradation, no…they're all clean," she replied. "Not even so much of a blue ultra-micro smudge."

"So, we have a message…but what kind of message? Is someone trying to get your attention? Or are you the eventual target? If so, how? We still don't know how this thing infected just these people."

"This lady I interviewed," Harri added, "she knew the two adults who were killed. And her daughter knew every one of the teens who were killed, at least up to when I talked with her."

"Interesting," Mark whispered. "Maybe they're behind this all?"

"I doubt it," Harri said. "I've seen enough fake emotions at my day job in Hollywood make-up and special effects. The daughter is practically ready for a deep psychotic plunge. My opinion is they may have a connection, possibly coincidentally, in knowing every single victim. But they just don't convey the markers of being murderers. I haven't filed that interview yet as I'm still reviewing it myself and checking for any possible social tie."

"Send me what you've got," Mark said.

"So, is this what you expected?" Mae asked.

"I suspected there would be a message at the cellular," he answered. "Everything else being unidentifiable, I deduced the clue would be under the cause, just not what the clue would be.

I'm shocked by what the clue is myself!"

Calvin stood and addressed the team. "I'm going to my office to research all my cases, see if anything pops out at me."

"Good idea," Mark said. "Harri, make another call on this lady and daughter, take Angela. Put on some pretty clothing instead, no uniforms. Make it more of a social visit, offer that progress is being made, and so on."

Angela and Harri both rose and said in unison, "Yes, sir," and departed the room, leaving Mark and Mae alone at the conference table.

"And next?" she asked when the door was closed.

"We wait," he said, "and talk things through." As always, Ensign Cutter was at the far end of the room, observing. "Cutter, We're gonna need three dark coffees, please."

"Aye, sir," she said, and departed the room. She returned a moment later with three large black coffees.

"And have a seat," he said to her as she served the cups. " You've listened to everything going on to this point, been running research lines for Oracle, so on and so on. Time to show off."

"'Show off', sir?"

Mark smiled. "Seriously? You think I don't know?"

"Know what?" Mae asked.

Cutter sat still, looking at Mark, mouth slightly ajar.

"She has an eidetic memory. It's why I had her assigned here as my assistant. Ensign Cutter can remember anywhere she's been at any time, what she's heard, what she's said and when…am I correct, Ensign?"

Cutter closed her mouth before answering, her tongue trying to moisten the inside of her closed mouth. "Yes, sir."

"So, with everything you've mentally recorded, what is your personal conclusion from all of it?"

"You want me to say it…now, sir?"

"Here and now."

"Yes, sir." She closed her eyes and wet her lips. "Sir, everything I've seen and heard to this point…leads me to believe that Agent Seeker is targeted to die a very excruciating death…"

CHAPTER 23

PRESSING

HOURS LATER

Y ou do realize that if anything happens to me, my wife will go on a killing spree."

Mark couldn't help but chuckle at Calvin's quip. "Yup, our Firebrand. You understand now why I haven't invited her to any team meetings, except the oldest core members."

Calvin followed Mark's steps as he poured them both a drink from his private bar and handed him a glass. "You knew all along?" Mark sat down on the couch in his office beside Calvin. "No, I know better than to ask such a question."

Mark said gently, "It's my job."

"Oh, crap," Calvin said with a chuckle as he sipped his drink. "After all these years I—we—have no idea where you learned to do things you do. And you know what? I've never seen you take a back seat to any mission before. Why are you pushing Angela so hard?"

Mark took a sip from his own glass without answering.

"What are you?" Calvin asked. "Are you even human? Are you some kind of plant within Task Force Division?" Calvin rotated in his seat to face Mark. "It's been, what, how many years? I've seen you disappear into mid-air, vanish from our scanners to re-appear somewhere else moments later? Just what are you?"

Mark smiled. "I'm a man just like you, Cal."

"With some inexplicable talents.

"And Angela has them, too."

"What?"

"Now's not the time for explanations," Mark said, rising.

"This is her first major test…along with us figuring out what's truly happening."

"Well, apparently I'm the target."

"Maybe," Mark replied.

"Oh, don't do your Spy shit on me, Mark," Calvin said, also rising. "Do you know what's really going on or not?"

Mark took another sip from his glass, then set it down on his bar surface. He stood silently for many seconds before he turned to Calvin. "There are a lot of things I can't tell you, old friend. There are some that I can. There are a lot of things progressing beyond your ken."

Calvin smiled as he shook his head "no". "Oh, no, don't you be all 'Confucius' on me. I've been on this team a hell of a lot longer than you have. Trust me, I've seen things across the world myself that would make your blood freeze…"

"Oh, I know all about them," Mark said, surprising Calvin.

"What the hell? How could you? A lot are redacted or not even recorded."

"It's—"

"No, don't even go there with that 'It's what I do' shit. Will you answer me or not?"

Mark sat in his desk chair and interlaced his fingers on its top. "Please, sit." After Calvin settled himself across from Mark, Mark said, "You have to accept that there are about to be a lot of changes happening, a lot of events, and Angela—Oracle—is about to be smack-dab in the middle of it all."

Calvin sat back in his seat. "Say, what? All these teen deaths and all, this is really about your daughter?"

"No," Mark answered, deadpan. "From everything at this point, this event is all about you."

"Well, just wonderful."

"And Angela."

Calvin laughed. "Always got to have a Jason involved."

"Hilarious," Mark replied. "And just what makes you say

that?"

Calvin sat back and said, "Seems like most of the time recently if there's been a problem it's been either The Spy or The Oracle who's been around for the rescue…"

Ho Choy sat on the ground beside Navy SEAL Lieutenant Mark Jason. "You know why you here?" he asked the young Navy officer.

"I've no doubt my father put me up to this," Mark replied.

"Good start," said Choy.

"So, why exactly am I here? I'm apparently not marked as AWOL or missing, otherwise I'd be picking up traffic on my disappearance."

"True," Choy said gently.

Mark sat for several moments, looking at his Chinese contact. "So why am I here? You going to kill me or something?"

Choy smiled. "Much worse…and much better…"

Mark explained to Calvin, "Try to understand. There are events always happening across the world, most minor, some important, a few REALLY important, which is where Task Force comes in. But remember the Task Force charter: the field team members are free to do their own things if they find an event requiring their talents without the rest of the team. Well, I'm an international businessman. International contacts, social connections, friends, et cetera. I've done decades of study in order to do the things I do…Angela is a spatial savant, and she is worlds beyond me in many respects. But like any rapidly advancing officer, she still needs training in her command position."

"Still doesn't answer my question," said Calvin. "What are YOU?"

Mark sighed. "Doesn't leave this office. I am a logical savant…amongst other things. Angela is a spatial savant. That's why Angela doesn't have a boyfriend or do much socializing; it's just not in her genetic makeup. As for me, well, I developed myself early in life to be better than the best, and that was due to my own Savant Syndrome, though that wasn't determined until my Navy assignment testing. Guess it runs in the family, poor Angela."

Calvin shook his head. "Shoulda guessed."

"Statistically, not within your logic threshold."

Calvin looked at Mark. "Ha ha, very funny."

Mark changed the subject finally. "Find anything in your old case files to determine who might be targeting you in this unusual way?"

"Dozens of possibilities," Calvin said. "And when I take out all the electronic talent abilities from everyone I've captured myself, alone or with the team, I fall back to just one name."

Mark closed his eyes and said, "The Talon."

Calvin nodded and said, "The Talon…"

CHAPTER 24

SIDETRACK

Mister Terrence looked at his watch, then placed a call on his cell phone. "Sir," he said when the call connected, "by now the encoded message should have been found."

The soft German voice responded, "It's a pity, true. Would be nice to know for certain. But no matter. Is the plan in place?"

"Yes, sir," he replied.

"Then proceed."

Amanda answered the knock at her door. She looked through the peephole and saw Mister Terrence standing outside. The door chain was still on from last night, so the door opened only a few inches. "I'm sorry, Mister Terrence, this is not a good time."

"I stopped at the restaurant first, just so you know I'm not trying to stalk you," he said as he removed his bowler. "I merely wanted to know if you were all right."

"No, I'm not, and I really don't want to talk about it."

"I understand." He turned to leave, but stopped short as he noticed her neck. "You aren't wearing the necklace I gave you?"

"That's a damn foolish question to ask at a time like this," Amanda answered, very irritated.

"My apologies. I shall leave you to tend to your matters. Good day, ma'am." He walked away without looking back, stopping at the elevator to wait for a car to take him to the street level.

Amanda closed the door. "Oh, God, if he wasn't so gorgeous, I'd shoot him…"

The next morning on the other side of town a school building not yet filled with children exploded…

CHAPTER 25

REVOLTING

This is getting to be a habit, being out in full view of everyone in uniform," Proteus said mostly to herself.

"This is an unusual situation," Spy answered. "Just stay badged up and don't talk to anyone outside the team." With that, he turned and walked to the fire chief on site. "Any ideas, Captain?" he asked in his usual electronically-altered voice.

"None, sir," Brian Meadows, the middle-aged chief replied. "We've got most of the hot spots contained, but obviously this is totally ruined."

"Hm," Spy said.

"Got something, boss," Proteus said aloud. The team's electronics expert pointed to several different locations. "This was definitely arson, with a dozen different detonation areas designed to go off at once."

"Why?" Spy asked.

Proteus smiled. "Isn't that your specialty?"

"Funny," he said, growling, "although true."

"I've marked all the D-sites for your eyes."

"Good work. Captain, I'll leave you to your work while I start mine, if you don't mind us stepping into the debris. I truly appreciate you allowing us to work beside your fine men."

"No problem," the fire chief said, "especially when we get a call from the governor, how can I refuse? By the way, who are you guys?"

"We're the ones who you've never seen before," Spy answered, "and who you'll forget were ever here."

He nodded in understanding and returned to working with his teams in completing putting out the remaining fires, hot spots, and smoking areas.

"Tactical, Spy," he said to his hood comm unit.

"Spy, Tactical," he heard in his ears.

"Record everything I see for immediate analysis, bring in the live crew."

"Roger," his Tactical assistant at Task Force Division said.

Spy stepped to the first area Proteus marked for him to review. He knelt to look at the burnt rubble and debris. Slowly he turned his head from side to side so that the view in his lenses could be fed to headquarters for live analysis.

However, after an hour of going to every marked location, he saw nothing out of the ordinary. "Tactical, anything?" he asked aloud.

"Still reviewing, Spy, but nothing unusual so far."

Damn, what a revolting development. "Discontinue feed, notify if you find anything, even an ant that's not supposed to be there."

"Roger. Tactical out."

Proteus approached him. "I've found a lot of cell phones, computers, CPUs, calculators…but nothing that spells out a source to me."

Spy shook his head. "Nothing out of the ordinary—wait. There was no one here when the building went out?"

"Correct," she said.

"Then…why were there cell phones?"

Proteus thought for a moment. "Could be they were confiscated and left behind?"

He turned his head to face her. "In this day and age? Would you leave your phone behind? Would your mom let your teacher keep it overnight?"

"Got your point."

"Show me the phone locations."

She guided him around the periphery of the ruins, pointing out every location of the phones, or what was left of them. "They're all exploded out from the same spots as the phones," he noted. He reached to pick up one from the debris. "Think you can dig into this thing, or any of the other phones, to check its settings?"

Proteus looked at what was left of the phone, then went back to him. "You've got to be kidding," she said, followed a moment later with, "I'm insulted it took you that long to ask!"

"I'm waiting," he replied, his voice in an obvious mimic of Vizzini from "The Princess Bride", spreading his arms like the character.

Proteus smiled and removed a couple pouches from her belt, opening them to reveal several micro-electric tools and tiny displays.

The fire chief noticed their concentration in that location and walked to them. "Find something?"

"An incongruity, and now testing," Spy said.

"What kind of—"

"Patience, Captain Meadows…she's working on it." He looked out over all the wreckage. "Where are the load-bearing beam locations of the school?"

Meadows tapped at his wired comm unit. "Who's got blueprints of this building?" he asked aloud.

"Yo!" answered one of the coordinators in the planning tent. A young man in a black t-shirt and firefighter pants jogged over to them. "Here you go."

Meadows said, "Barney, do you know where the load-bearing sections are on this thing?"

"Yeah," Barney answered. He pointed his finger to each spot on the diagram, saying "here" at each one.

Spy was the first to react. "That's every location a cell phone was found."

"A remotely controlled multi-detonation," Harri amended as she approached. "I managed to get into three of the phones' memories, they all got a call from the same number at the same time as the explosion. The rest were too far gone."

Meadows countered with, "But we've no sign of detonation residue."

"Nitro?" Proteus suggested.

"Nitroglycerine," Spy agreed. "Can detonate when agitated, such as when shook—"

"—from a phone's vibrate-only setting," she added, nodding.

"And no residue," Meadows said.

"And likely nothing in the phones that will lead us to who is responsible for this."

"Boss, why do this BEFORE school? Wouldn't the arsonist want this explosion to be a major loss of life thing?" Proteus asked.

Spy shook his head. "No, I think this was intentional…wanting our attention, get us out in the open."

"But why?"

"Why, indeed…"

CHAPTER 26

WHY

It makes sense," Calvin said at the conference room assembly. "My name in microscopic code, killing random teenagers to get our attention then blowing up a school to draw us out…it's like this was all orchestrated just for us."

"Plus, the mysterious 'Terrence'," Angela added.

"The real question is, 'Why?'," Harri said.

Mark sat at the head of the table as usual, listening. "The Talon is off the grid," he stated professionally. "Doesn't mean he's not involved and makes me think this Terrence is an employee or such."

"Stepping outside the box, Daddy?" Angela asked.

"It's a supposition that, in my opinion, makes the most sense. Doesn't mean it's right, nor wrong, just is." Mark sat forward to lean on the table. "Harri, you reported that this mother and daughter knew all the victims?"

"Correct, boss."

"Did the daughter happen to attend this particular school?"

Harri's eyes widened. "As a matter of fact—"

"Let's go back to them, then. There had to be something that happened to them right before all this started. Were they blackmailed? Or were they paid to do something?"

"I already checked their bank account," Harri said, "with their permission via email. There's nothing out of the ordinary there. The mom's survivor's benefit, her regular payroll…that's it. And no trace of them spending any more than they take in."

Mae commented, "Still doesn't mean they couldn't be on the take."

"Doesn't mean they are, either," said Angela.

"I believe they are innocent," Harri interrupted. "I sat with them, I talked with them…they're both tortured about all this."

"Then we take your opinion as primary," Mark announced, "but they are still connected to this whole thing."

"Agreed. But, how?"

"There has to be something," Calvin said, "something we're missing."

"Staring at us, mocking us," Mark mused.

"Let me go back to them," Harri said, rising. "We are missing something, and I'm going to find out. Angela, wanna ride shotgun?"

"Sounds good."

"Dress in street clothes," Mark ordered, "no more undue attention in the blacks. But be armed and commed."

"Roger," both women said in unison as they left.

Mae asked when the door closed, "You know what she has in mind?"

Mark tilted his head, smiling. "Of course, not…"

Amanda looked through her apartment peephole to see the short blond agent with a taller brunette beside her. She opened the door, saying, "Hello, Agent Proteus."

"Mrs. Curry, do you have a little more time to talk with us? This is Agent Oracle."

"You do have some unusual names," Amanda said as she opened the door to give them entry. "Please, make yourselves comfortable. How can I help you today?"

"Is Dagen doing any better?" Oracle asked.

"More upset than ever, with her school destroyed," Amanda replied. "She's taken to staying in her room all the time now, like a hermit, lights out…"

"Major depressive disorder," Oracle added. "Not unusual, considering what's going on. You may want to—"

"Not the time," Proteus interrupted. "We're getting some pieces put together, Mrs. Curry, and think you and Dagen may be in the middle of it all."

"Us? How? We don't do anything…"

"Well, we've been trying to track all that's been going on. Every single victim has been someone you or Dagen know."

Amanda's jaw dropped. "Are you thinking we…that we had anything to do with this? We're as shocked with all this as everyone else!"

"Not exactly," Oracle said. "Not so much the cause…as the source."

Amanda looked back and forth at both agents. "I—I don't understand. What do you mean?"

Proteus cleared her throat. "This is way out of left field, but…have you ever met a man calling himself 'Terrence'?"

Her face blanched white. "Mister Terrence?"

The agents looked at each other. "You have met him?"

"A few times. He showed up at my diner one day, out of nowhere…he's very, very handsome, incredible English accent, muscular—"

"Got it," said Proteus.

"And the most courteous, gentle man I've ever met. I'm sorry, but he makes me feel so…um…"

"Got it," said Proteus again. "Sounds like a dreamboat."

"Oh, you have no idea, ladies…he's just…perfect…"

"Have you ever had relations with him?" Oracle asked, ending the swooning moment.

Amanda was shocked. "None of your business!... But no. Haven't been that interested in anyone since my husband died overseas. But sometimes I do miss the attention."

"So, no communicability," Proteus whispered to Oracle. "Have you seen him anytime besides the restaurant?"

"He's come here a couple times," Amanda replied. "Came with some beautiful flowers."

"Any other gifts?"

"Um…well… he came by my apartment to deliver a cash tip he didn't leave at the restaurant."

"What did you do with that cash?" Oracle asked.

"Deposited it, of course."

"Was your teller Patti Key?"

"Why…yes!"

Oracle removed her phone from her pocket and made a call. "Spy, Oracle. Examine the money from Patti Key's tell… should still be on lockdown."

With the precautions already in place at the bank, Patti's till and all her drawers were locked down as her death was investigated.

The sight of the fully-masked Spy and Hawaiian agent Hunter disrupted the customers and staff of Patti's bank, their shields on display as they proceeded unrestricted to Patti's till locked in the safe.

Once they were in private, Spy activated the team's private channel. "Okay, Oracle, what are we looking for?"

"Examine the cash in her till, look for any contagion."

"Run the J-167 scanner," Spy said to Hunter.

"Roger." She reached into a satchel she carried in with her. She withdrew a handheld scanner that could read biometric contaminations on any surface. "Running now."

"Any time," Spy said. "We're interrupting bank time."

"It runs at its own pace for a mobile system."

"I know."

Several minutes pass as the mobile scanner reads the surfaces of every piece of money in the teller's cabinet. When it completed its task and automatically shut down, she said, "Everything is clean."

"What???"

"This money, paper and coin, is perfectly safe to return to the general distribution."

"Run it again."

Hunter complied and ran it a second time…

…and a third time…

…even a fourth time.

"What the hell are we missing?" Spy finally said. "Proteus, Spy. Are you sure this equipment is operating—"

"—I am so insulted you would question my stuff," she said in his ear. "I will guarantee that my equipment works perfectly any time and every time."

Hunter, connected to the network feed, simply shrugged her shoulders.

"Shit," Spy said. "Okay, lock it back up. Hunter, tell the bank manager to keep this isolated for the time being, then meet me back at base."

"Roger," she said, and began packing her equipment…and saw that her team leader was gone. "I hate it when he does that…"

An hour later, Angela was in her father's office at Task Force Division. They both had a tumbler of scotch in their hands as they sat in his office chairs, still in their uniforms but without their gun belts on nor their glasses and hood (in his case).

"We're still missing something," Mark said.

"No shit," Angela said as she sipped at her drink.

"Language, Commander."

"I still don't give a shit, SIR," she said sarcastically. "Actually, I do. This is really pissing me off."

"I do understand," Mark replied, sipping his drink.

They sat in their chairs, lost in their respective thoughts on the current crisis.

All the data swirled in Angela's mind. Her mental capacity as a spatial savant saved many people over the years since her permanent assignment from the Navy to Task Force Division, yet she felt empty from not being able to solve this one mystery which had already taken many lives and caused a school's destruction.

She was barely aware of him refilling her tumbler. "I don't need it—"

"Drink it, that's an order."

She sipped her refilled glass. "Why?"

"Because I see the smoke coming out of your damn ears."

"Ha, ha," she said as she raised her glass before taking another sip. "If you were my age I'd say you're trying to get me drunk to take advantage of me."

"I happen to know that NO one has taken advantage of you," he countered.

She sat erect and scowled at him. "THAT'S NONE OF YOUR DAMN BUSINESS!" she shouted, "even if you are my father!!!"

"Am I wrong?" he asked calmly.

"Well, I—that is, I…well, son of a bitch!"

"Take another sip."

"I did!"

"Then another," he said.

She took another sip. "You been spying on me, Agent Spy?"

"Nope. I know you better than you know yourself." He leaned forward to look at her. "Ever since you were assigned here, you've been pulling fourteen-hour days, even coming in on weekends. You have NO personal life! It's here or sleep. That's all you do, Angel! Why?"

"I—I—" Angela had no better answer. "This is a helluva time to come at me about my private life, Daddy—"

"You have no private life, Angel," Mark rebutted. "Even though that Jergens boy turned out to be gay, you could have gone after some other young fella."

"I haven't been interested," Angela said. "I like my work. I like my assignment, and the team I command."

"That's not all there is to life, baby," Mark said.

"It's all I need."

"Is it?"

"My little apartment is fine. My car is fine. What I have as a Task Force Field Team operative is fine."

"So, when are you gonna get a boyfriend and get laid?"

"DADDY!!!"

Mark couldn't help but laugh loud and hard.

"Seriously! That is NOT something a father should say to his daughter!!!"

Mark gently ended his laughter and sat back. "Listen, little girl. And then forget what I say. You have a major future in store if you continue this track. But you have one major demerit: no social score. The thing about being an agent—especially a Task Force agent—is the ability to adapt to any situation. You have deprived yourself of the social atmosphere so that you can be anyone, anywhere." He stopped for another sip. "You are one of the smartest people to ever walk the Earth in its history—" he leaned toward her "—and one of the most stupid."

"I—I—"

"Stow it, Commander," he continued, changing his tone. "Also telling you something to forget; you will be the next commander of the Field Team, whether I retire or am killed on assignment."

"That's not what I—"

"Of course, that's what you want," he interrupted. "You reached the rank of Commander in less than half the time of anyone in your graduating corps. That's because of YOU. And you've built an incredible department here, helped saved many lives because of what you've got up there." He pointed at her head. "You are one of the most incredible people to ever walk the planet. But maybe you need to start feeling stupid."

Angela opened her mouth to reply but stopped. She began thinking at her unique top speed, and Mark saw her eyes glaze over in the process. He sat back with his drink lifted for a fuller sip, waiting for her to process the conversation. *One of my greatest pleasures,* he thought, *making her think about something she doesn't want to.*

A trademark of both Mark and Angela Jason was the catatonic state when they went into deep introspection and calculation, although Mark was more frequent at such interruptions. Many minutes passed as he watched Angela process their conversation.

Finally, Angela moved and said, "Assemble the team..."

CHAPTER 27

WHAT

I am so pissed at my father," the tipsy Angela announced to the assembled Task Force team. "Getting me so drunk last night. And my apologies to Firebrand for not including her in the last couple meetings. I discounted your contributions to the team."

"No problem," said Stephanie. "I'll kill you later."

"Accepted," Angela replied. "Anyway, we saw the major clue, but didn't do anything with it. The nodules that spelled out Seeker's agent name."

Calvin replied, "But there was nothing that connected me to this—whatever it is. Simply markers in virus nodules."

"And we have this mother-daughter factor," Angela continued. "They knew every victim…in fact, in contact with each one."

"We know that much," said Harri. "They admitted as much, but that's all the connection we could determine. Nothing unusual."

"And we have the mysterious 'Terrence'," Angela said. "He's been in touch with the Curry family. After his first contact with them, people they knew started dying.”

“Point!” said Mark loudly. “You’re preaching facts we have assembled. Where is the direction of proof?”

“Dammit,” Angela said. “The direction…the connection…I missed it…”

“You haven’t missed it,” Calvin offered optimistically. “On the contrary, you’ve provided a track to investigate.”

“Hm?” she asked back.

“Is there a connection between this ‘Terrence’, and the sudden deaths, and the school explosion? Inference seems to think so. Proof is sorely lacking.”

Mark watched silently as the discussion ensued. Angela said, “It’s my job to provide the information—”

“—and it’s my job to find the villain,” said Calvin. “Hunter’s job to track down the villain, Proteus’ job to discover the villain…what’s your point?”

“As you were,” Mark ordered calmly.

Angela sat in her seat and stayed silent for a couple minutes.

“We know our specialties,” Mark said calmly, “but everyone is trained in multiple abilities, Angela. Stop feeling beaten and open your eyes to everything.”

As Angela thought internally, Harri wrote a note in her notebook and turned the page face-down. They all waited on Angela.

Only a couple minutes passed until Angela said, “We need to examine the mother and daughter.”

Mark nodded at his daughter as she rose and left the conference room. He looked at Harri as she lifted her hidden note which read:

“Mom and daughter are key…”

CHAPTER 28

CHANCE

Days passed with no further incident, neither death nor destruction. To the public, it seemed that the crisis had ended.

At Task Force Division, the field team agents examined their evidence as deeply as they could. Despite confirming that the school destruction was definitely man-made, confirming who was responsible remained elusive.

Mark knew that Amanda and Dagen were the key to the entire affair, but there was no concrete proof. Angela continued the dark web and matrix searches for any mention of them or of the plot, with no results.

He stepped into Angela's office. "I have to head back to Richmond and do some work at Jason Enterprises. Only so much that I can do remotely."

"And I'm sure Mom misses you, too," she replied. She rose to give him a hug goodbye, with a kiss on his bearded cheek for good measure. "I love you, Daddy."

"Love you, too, Angel," he said as he hugged her. "You know I'm so very proud of you."

She pulled back, a slight grin on her face. "Hold the praise until after I solve this thing. You know how I hate undeserved praise."

"Even so," he replied. "Just keep me in the loop. Bye."

"Bye, Daddy."

Mark departed through the back-office corridor to his waiting driver to take him to the Jason Enterprises jet waiting at Dulles Airport.

"Okay, you electronic gremlins, let's have a little chat…"

Hours later Angela, dressed in civilian clothing again, stopped at Harri's office door. "Feel up to another visit to our ladies? I've got an idea."

Harri rose to her feet. "Sure, let me get my shoes on—"

"—and bring a portable med kit…"

"Again?" Amanda asked.

"This might be the last time," Oracle said, "or, honestly, it could be the first of many more."

"You real-life agents are worse than any on TV!" Amanda said in exasperation. She waved her arm. "Come on in and pardon the mess."

"No, worries," Proteus said. "Is your daughter here?"

"In her bedroom."

"We'll need her in a few minutes," Oracle said. "May we sit?"

"Sure. Would you like some coffee? I really need some myself."

"We're good, thank you," Proteus replied. "Mind if I set

up my equipment here?"

"Equipment for what?"

"Possibly some answers," Oracle answered.

The agents sat in the living room barrel seats while Amanda returned with her coffee. As she set it on the coffee table, the necklace around her neck escaped the confines of her button-down uniform blouse.

It was the talon necklace.

Oracle was the first to notice. "Mrs. Curry, where did you get that charm?" That caught Proteus' attention, and her mouth opened.

"Actually, Mister Terrence gave it to me as part of a large tip."

Proteus inquired, "Has anyone touched that besides you?"

"Just Dagen. Why?"

Proteus reached into her equipment bag and pulled out two pairs of medical gloves. Both agents immediately pulled them on. "Would you mind handing it to me?"

As Amanda reached behind her neck she asked, "Sure…this is really getting strange."

The agent gently took the charm and necklace in her protected hand, placed it on a scanner screen from her bag, and turned it on. "This will take a little bit to process. We need to take blood samples from both of you now."

"What? This is absolutely—"

"I have the medical knowledge to do it safely right here," Oracle said. "I'll take yours first, and let Proteus start analyzing it, while I get a sample from your daughter."

Amanda could only puff in exasperation as she rolled up her sleeve. "I hope this is all worth it."

"Us, too, ma'am," said Oracle. "There are a lot of people hoping the same thing."

A minute later Proteus took the sample of Amanda's blood to start the analysis, and Oracle went to Dagen's room.

The teenager was buried in her blankets on her bed. The

room was dark, save for the hall light that shone on her face; there were many dried tear marks on her cheeks. "Hey, Miss Dagen," Oracle said softly. "It's me, Agent Oracle. Mind if I sit with you?"

Dagen opened her eyes slightly, swollen from all her crying. "If you want."

"How are you doing, sweetheart?"

"I'm so scared," Dagen said softly. "I keep thinking I could be next."

"I'm sure you won't be," Oracle said.

"How do you know?"

"Fair question. Let's just say for now that we're working on a new line of thought. But to help, I need to take a blood sample from you. Is that okay?"

Dagen reached her hand out of the covers and wiped her eyes. "I hate needles."

Oracle chuckled. "Makes two of us, and I've had a lot of shots in my years." The teen sat up, and as she was wearing a T-shirt, she didn't need to roll up her sleeve. Oracle tied a rubber tourniquet on the teen's bicep. "This will sting for only a moment," she added as she wiped the girl's inner elbow. She then stuck in the needle, quickly drew a sample, undoing the tourniquet at the same time. The syringe filled, Oracle removed it, and put a cotton swab on the needle site. "Hold that for me?" As Dagen put her other hand on the swab, Oracle walked the sample to Proteus. She returned quickly and showed the band-aid in her hand. "Thought you might like a special bandage."

"Oh, cool!" Dagen smiled. She watched as Oracle placed a Star Trek-themed band aid on the extraction point. "Thank you!"

"Thought you might like that. Now, you just get yourself better. I hope to see you well soon."

"I'll try." Dagen snuggled back into her covers as Oracle closed the door.

As she turned from closing the bedroom door, she almost ran into her partner. Proteus spoke softly, "This is good or bad, depending on your point of view…these two are our Typhoid

Marys…"

CHAPTER 29

CONFIRM

Their apartment was sealed by CDC staff as Amanda and Dagen were dressed in airtight suits with attached oxygen tanks and escorted in a black van to the Task Force medical building. The CDC began an intensive examination, along with Task Force medical staff, of the apartment, studying each surface and item for additional signs of the contamination Proteus found in her onsite exam.

The mother and daughter were escorted inside a sealed room after the van came to an eventual stop. They were surrounded by men and women in hazmat suits, with Agent Proteus leading them.

Proteus waved them into a beautifully decorated room and gestured for them to sit on either the couch or chairs. She tapped the side of her head to open a channel so they could hear her. "Amanda, Dagen, you're going to receive the best care in the world here. But first I'm going to need you both to strip off everything and put on these medical togs," she instructed, pointing at two sets of clothes and sneakers. "We need to test your clothing and jewelry."

"Will we get it back?" Amanda asked.

"After we've run out tests and purification procedures. Similar work is being done at your home…and don't worry, everything will be just as you found it when you get home."

"Not 'if'?" Dagen asked.

"No," said Proteus. "We're not like those fed types in the movies." She moved to the open door and closed it, flipping three switches by the door frame. They all heard a medium-loud hiss, and when it stopped Proteus said, "Ladies, I'm going to remove your air suits, and then you can get undressed."

"With you watching?" said Dagen, shocked.

"Well, I'm a girl just like you, so it's not like I'm a threat to you…but I need to take each piece of clothing you remove and place it in a security box to go to the lab, so no dropping anything on the floor." She stepped to the table with their sterile clothes and removed two sheets of paper, poster-board sized. "When you remove your footwear, please step on this paper until you have your temporary sneakers on. Then I will pack up those papers as well."

"Kinda overboard, don't ya think?" the young girl asked.

"Kinda doing what we have to, to keep you and your mom alive. Besides, you have no idea some of the things we've had to go through over the years."

"Love to listen," Amanda replied.

"Sorry, no security clearance," Proteus said with a smile.

As the mother and daughter slowly removed each piece of their clothing, Proteus took each and carefully folded it to place in one of two sterile boxes: one for Amanda, one for Dagen. As she was folding Dagen's bra for her box, Proteus' eye caught a flash of gold in Amanda's direction. She turned to reach for Amanda's bra when her eyes concentrated on the mother's neck. Reflexively, Amanda crossed her arms to cover her breasts. "What?" Amanda asked.

Proteus stepped in front of her. Pointing at the necklace in her gloved hand, she asked, "Where did you get that?"

"This charm? It was a tip gift from Mister Terrence—"

"Oracle, Proteus," the agent said aloud as she closed the channel to isolate Amanda and Dagen.

"Proteus, Oracle, go," she heard in her ear.

"Confirming The Talon is behind this all," Proteus said. "The mother is wearing a standard talon token…"

CHAPTER 30

ASSUMPTION

S On of a bitch, I knew it," Calvin said in the conference room. "I knew it!"

"Ever since your name showed up in the imaging, I felt it myself," Stephanie affirmed. "You were the only law enforcer to have ever captured him, and it was only a matter of time before he lashed out for revenge."

"But is this really revenge?" Angela asked. "Aside from naming you, there hasn't been any action against you."

With Mark away, Calvin sat in the team leader chair, with Tom to the side as always. "Very true," he admitted.

"Just an attention-getter," said Harri. "You and Stephanie were together when you arrested him; while he didn't mention her, I feel that it's for both of you."

Stephanie looked at Calvin from her seat. "That's true, Cal."

"Has there been any other activity since the school explosion?" Calvin asked.

The agents looked at each other. "Actually, no," Mae answered.

"So, what's the connection to all this?" he asked. "I have no doubt this is all connected. The Talon is not one to just kill and destroy; there is a meaning to it. Ideas?"

For several seconds there was silence. Finally, Angela said, "Sorry, guys, I've got nothing."

"All this technology we have," Harri added, "and nothing. We need the Adam West Batcomputer!"

"Wait!" Angela burst out. "Maybe we're being too smart for our own good. Let's do it Adam West Bat-style!"

"What?" Mae asked.

"Let's pull the basic info together. So, have fourteen total victims, one still alive. One and thirteen. 113? 131? 311? Only numerical combinations."

"I follow now," Mae said. "So maybe that's a house or building number?"

"Good," said Calvin. "And my name?"

"There's no 'Seeker' street in Centreville, where all this is happening," Angela reported.

"Agent?" Harri asked.

"No 'Agent' street."

"Secret Agent?" Stephanie offered.

"No…well, there is a 'Secret' street," Angela said. "It's a residential street, all numbered in the 300s."

"Holy secret hideaway, Batman!" Harri exclaimed.

"Seriously?" Calvin asked. "Is it that easy to deduce, using a sixty-year-old superhero show's style of calculation?"

"Got any better idea?" Angela countered.

"Okay, fine," Calvin conceded. "Stephanie, you're with me. The rest of you, requisition regular vehicles from the motor pool and park nearby, arrive at staggered times, no pattern. Then we'll arrive at a random time later in a company car."

"Cutter, transmit to Mark what we're running with," Angela ordered Mark's ever-present silent assistant.

"Aye, sir," she said, rising to go to her desk.

"Let's move, people," Calvin ordered.

As the team disbanded to prepare for the mission, Stephanie said, "I hope we're not shooting ourselves in the back with this."

"Makes two of us," Calvin said…

CHAPTER 31

TARGET

Several hours later Seeker drove his car onto Secret Lane and parked in front of house 311, a modest middle-class house with one floor, front door in the middle of the street facing side, and lots of trees and shrubs. "Here we are, Firebrand," he said formally, fully expecting his voice would already be monitored and not wanting to give away the team members' positions, let alone their presence nearby.

"Did it once, ready for the repeat?" she asked.

"Not like we had anything else to do today," he replied. "I'm sure we're expected, so let's get to it."

They exited his car and walked across the grass to the front door. Both were in their standard black uniforms and fully armed. He knocked.

A large burly bald man opened the door; he was at least six inches taller than Seeker. "I think we're expected," the agent said.

"Weapons," the guard demanded, holding out his hands.

"Yeah, we have weapons," Seeker deadpanned as they walked past him into the house. The guard tried to stop them by grabbing their shoulders, but Seeker turned around to give him an easy karate throw out into the lawn and closed the door after him. "Too easy," Seeker said.

"But of course," said a British-accented deep voice. "Please, come in and make yourselves comfortable."

The duo entered the house's living room to meet a dozen more guards pointing semi-automatic rifles at them, and a muscular black man in a three-piece suit at the opposite end of the room sipping tea.

"You're not Talon," Firebrand said.

"No, I'm not," the man said, setting his cup on its saucer and rising. "You may call me Mister Terrence." He stepped forward to request her hand, which she offered, and he kissed, then shook Seeker's hand. "So long as you keep your weapons where they are you will not be hurt and will be free to go when we are concluded."

The agents sat in different seats, creating a triangle with Terrence as he, too, sat in his chair and reached for his teacup. "Tactical positions, very good. Increasing your survival percentage should combat break out. Again, not necessary in this visit."

"So, what is the purpose of this visit? And why all the death and destruction to get our attention for simply a meeting?"

"A test," Terrence said. "Merely a test."

"All that for a damn TEST???" Firebrand shouted angrily. The guards turned their guns to her, but Terrence waved them off.

"Yes, my dear," he replied. "The Talon wanted to know how your team would respond to a major threat. You did deduce this location a bit sooner than expected, however. Very impressive."

"We went a little West on that," Seeker answered.

"A little 'West'? Interesting, I'll have to learn about that technique. Anyway, I have to express being impressed with your organization. It's taken me years to even figure out how to bring you out into the open, as you are all very expert on staying in the shadows."

"Subjecting a mother and daughter to such emotional pain?" Firebrand growled. "And all the families who will be burying their loved ones? Children an+d mothers?"

"Casualties of war," Terrence said calmly.

"We are not at war," Seeker said.

"Oh, but you are!" Terrence replied. "The day you captured Talon in Buenos Aires was the day it was declared. By ruining his perfect record, you cost him quite a few contracts, necessitating him staying behind bars longer than desired. But he lived comfortably while incarcerated until he was ready to leave. And while he has been rebuilding his reputation since escaping, it has been my sole job to track you down." He sipped. "While I have now determined there are six of you, I still have yet to actually identify who you are as a team or unit."

Firebrand winked at Seeker. "We are the ones who don't exist."

Seeker did a "thumbs-up" gesture to her.

Terrence chuckled. "Entertaining, to be sure," he said. "And not surprising. I know that there are many mystery groups in your government; every government across the planet has such mystery groups. I was just hoping to know more about yours…but I know that won't happen any time soon. No matter," he paused, standing, "while you, Seeker, are the one who is desired, your partner here is as valuable. Please accompany me." He led them to the back yard, which had a privacy fence all around to conceal the open hatch into an underground area. "Please, proceed, and again a reminder to leave your weapons where they are, as there are armed guards awaiting you below."

"Thanks," Seeker said, as he and his partner took the steps to descend into the ground.

"And I just washed this suit," she added.

At the bottom of the hidden steps, they found themselves in a submerged hallway. "Please proceed," Terrence said. The long well-lit hallway ended at an intersection of three more halls.

"Straight," Terrence prompted. The agents, Terrence, and guards continued straight to a door at the end, which opened automatically upon their approach. The room was a luxuriously decorated office, with a blond-haired man sitting at a desk. "Welcome at last, Monsieur Chercheur."

"TALON!"…

CHAPTER 32

REVEAL

Good to see you and your lovely partner again," said the international terrorist and extortionist known as The Talon. "Please, do come in and sit down. Would you care for refreshments?" he asked in his soft German-accented voice.

As the agents sat in the chairs in front of his desk, both said, "No, thank you."

"Now, then," Talon continued, "you probably wonder why I requested your presence."

"Still figuring the 'requested' part," said Seeker. "You could have done it less cold-blooded."

Talon nodded his head. "It would not have been as much fun, however."

"Ha ha."

"American humor, so staid. But let me put it this way: you cost me quite a bit, capturing me years ago, so this was my way of evening the score."

Firebrand began to move, but Seeker grabbed her arm. "No," he said simply.

"My dear," said Talon, "last time we met you were an FBI agent, and now you're part of your man's team? Appears I have missed much."

"Nothing that would interest you," she replied.

"Perhaps, perhaps not," Talon answered.

"So just exactly why are we here?" Seeker demanded.

"Patience, patience, my friend. You see," Talon started, rising to his feet to circle around his desk, "you are the only agent to have ever captured me. And while I have friends in prisons across the globe for a just-in-case event, my total escape was thanks to your fellow agents taking down The Black Widow. So, I'm going to show you a courtesy, as professional rivals."

Seeker crossed his legs at the knees and sat back in his chair, pretending to accept this casual conversation offer. "Oh? Do tell. I'm all ears."

"You attempt to amuse me. You need much practice, sir." Talon turned to his desk and lifted the folder in the top's center and handed it to Seeker. "Before you open it, I am giving you a challenge. In that folder is my next contracted target. I have accepted it, and I will succeed. I am giving you the opportunity to stop me."

Both the agents' eyebrows rose in unison. "What makes you think I can't stop you right now?" Seeker asked.

"I think the dozen guards behind you would fill you both with much lead before you could, how do you say, 'slap leather'."

"Damn, man, you've thought of everything."

"Well, not quite. You see, this is the biggest contract of my career...and the last. Mister Seeker, your English name version, I have a secret I'm going to share with you. You might enjoy it, but not after I give you the caveats."

"We're on pins and needles," Firebrand muttered.

"Ah, agent...what is your name, anyway?"

"Unimportant."

"Very well, Agent Unimportant. Seeker...I am dying."

"Oh, joy! Where's the champagne?"

"Ah, not so fast," Talon said, smiling. "My successor has already been chosen, so on the day I pass this person will step up immediately as the new Talon. When, I will not say. But the Talon Empire will never die."

"So, what's the point?"

"The point is that many operations are already active to complete this contract. I'm giving you and your team the challenge to stop me if you can."

Suddenly from behind the agents there was an explosion of gunfire, and Talon's guards rapidly fell, some firing their weapons into the ceiling as they died. Seeker and Firebrand never moved, keeping their eyes on Talon.

"Are we late?" Oracle asked as she approached through the bodies. "We took that left turn at Albuquerque and got lost." She held her gun aimed at Talon.

Spy joined her side. "And the rest of your army upstairs is either dead or captured with the rest of our team watching over them."

"Well," Talon said, "it's an honor to meet Seeker's crew at last."

Seeker thumbed his hand toward Spy. "Actually, he's the boss."

"Ah, well played, sir. Well played."

"You're under arrest for murder, arson, and terrorism," Spy said, beginning to approach Talon with handcuffs from his belt. "You and your English boy here."

Terrence lifted his teacup in a toast.

"Yes, true…but in all the fun you forgot something else very important."

Oracle spoke first. "Shit, the mother and daughter!"

"The final card to play," Talon said.

Spy reached forward with his muscled left arm, grabbed Talon's shirt and jacket in a powerful fist, and lifted him off his feet. "The cure," Spy growled in his electronic deep voice.

"Oh, yes, it is here," Talon said.

"Mind if I ask a question before you turn him into so much pulp?" Oracle asked. Spy nodded. "The talon charm confirmed you were behind everything, we found the virus nodules in their blood, but they never had any symptoms, so how did they spread it?"

"IF you don't mind, sir?" Talon said to Spy, who lowered him to his feet. "Do you mind if I sit? I don't have the stamina I used to."

Now Seeker raised his weapon from his belt. "Keep your hands where I can see them and move cautiously."

"Of course," Talon replied. Hands raised; he circled back to his desk chair. "It was a genetic assault weapon."

"What?" asked Oracle.

Talon took a deep relaxing breath. "Several months ago, when I began this plan I had one of my subordinates go to her restaurant frequently, watching for when she rested and ate. After one day when her daughter joined her, he found their refuse in the trash and brought samples back to my lab in Argentina. My team crafted a special virus to which only they were immune and only they could spread."

"But it didn't spread like COVID or any other epidemic or pandemic. How did those victims catch it?" Oracle asked.

"It was a one-generation-only spread, and only to the people the mother and daughter actually touched, skin to skin. But those infected could not spread it, as it was not matched to their genetic codes and the nodules attacked their new hosts as any infection would, and it died in their own blood after they died."

"One still lives."

"That was intended. I have a doctor on staff there who gave that victim a lesser cure serum just to keep her alive enough to give you part of the clue to find me. She'll live when she gets the cure, plus the mother and daughter."

"And just where exactly is it?"

"If I may?" Talon moved his hand slowly into his front jacket pocket to remove a small glass vial, less than half the size of his fingertip…and which he pressed between his thumb and forefinger. "This is the only and total cure for the ladies. I shall depart and leave you this vial, or you can arrest me and I destroy it with just a little more pressure…your choice."

"Son of a bitch," Seeker growled. "Should have anticipated that."

Spy held out his left hand. "Done. My word that you will go."

"I like dealing with you, masked man," Talon said as he started to reach for Spy's gloved hand, but stopped, "However, I now know just how strong you are, and you could probably crush my hand without breaking the vial. No, friends, I am going to place the vial on my desk and bid you adieu." He placed the vial down as he said, and he and his chair dropped into the floor with a replacement plate sliding into place.

"Holy Wo Fat, Batman!" Oracle exclaimed.

Spy turned off his voice modulator. "Should have expected that," he said more to himself. "Something to remember for next time."

Oracle picked up the vial gently and placed it in a cushioned pouch on her belt. "I'll get this back to headquarters ASAP."

Spy nodded, and she departed. "As for you, Mister Terrence, you're headed for a long interrogation and incarceration.

"Not unexpected, sir," Terrence said. He downed the rest of his tea, stood and placed his hands behind his back for the handcuffs.

"Very affable of you," Spy said. "Firebrand, would you like to take him in?"

"My pleasure, boss," she said. She cuffed him and led him to the exit.

"We heard everything on the comms," Spy said to Seeker. "Did he indicate any signs or such that weren't audible?"

"Nothing," Seeker said. "Only what you heard. And we're

back to square one."

"Not exactly," Spy replied. He held up a non-company cell phone in his right hand. "I palmed it from his jacket when I picked him up. Put it in a Faraday bag in your car to keep him from remotely deleting it when he realizes I have it and get it back to headquarters for immediate analysis."

"Righto," said Seeker. He took off to follow Firebrand.

As he exited, Spy called out to Seeker, "You two did great today."

"Thanks, boss…not so bad yourself!" Seeker caught up to Firebrand and together they departed with Mister Terrence in custody as Task Force cleaners in gray uniforms arrived to begin marking the scene, collecting weapons, and other tasks.

Spy and Oracle walked together in the hallway back to the stairs to the yard. "Well, how'd I do?" she asked casually. "Good enough to be a permanent field team member?"

He stopped and faced her. "Taking on the task of finding a man-made virus, leading the entire medical staff plus CDC members, leading the field team in this crisis, et cetera?"

"Well, yeah, kinda…"

"Well, let me think…I believe I can score you in this test under fire…Not bad, Commander, not bad at all…"

JACK GANNON

While Jack usually writes with co-author Cyndi Williams-Barnier, receiving 5-star awards for three of their joint novels, and one 5-star award for his solo Christmas book, "I Walked In Santa's Boots", which was the book that launched YBR Publishing. They have four other books together, and after a few planning sessions he is at work on the next two in their "Task Force" series.

Jack's career was in print media, starting as a carrier for The Beaufort Gazette before a summer job as an intern reporter. He later returned to the Gazette as the mailroom supervisor, working his way up in the Circulation Department to Circulation System Manager for both the Gazette and The Island Packet. After 23 years in management, Jack entered retirement.

From 1993 to 2016, Jack also appeared as Santa Claus for Beaufort, SC, and the surrounding areas of upper Beaufort County. Although he retired from the couple dozen-plus major events he anchored in Beaufort County every year as St. Nick, he continued to appear at a couple smaller events in neighboring Jasper County for children's events as well as Toys For Tots. Jack was given a Toys For Tots pin from attending US Marines for his years helping to gather toys for needy children. His "Santa's Boots" book showcases his over two decades of major event appearances. He finally hung up his Red Coat after 30 years.

When he relaxes, it's with his wife Mendy, Pomeranian Kieran, and Russian Blue Mister Grey on the couch…

CYNDI WILLIAMS-BARNIER

I grew up in what was once the small town of Beaufort, S.C., with a population of approximately 6,300 in the early 1960s. Our small town now has a grandiose population of nearly 13,000, and the county 191,000! Things sure have changed!

After graduating from Beaufort High School, I went on to the University of S.C.-Beaufort studying Advanced Composition. From there I worked for S.C. Probation, Parole, and Pardons. After a 20-year career with the Beaufort County Emergency Management Division, I entered retirement. About the same time, we moved to our retirement house in Ridgeland, S.C.

In retirement I caught up with my dear friend Jack Gannon from Beaufort High School, where we often talked about writing books and were even planning out our storyline and characters for a book that we wanted to write. As fate would have it, we lost touch with each other after graduation. Fast forward some 32 years, we reconnected and finally began writing the book we talked about so long ago. To date we've written nine books in total with more to come!

In 2016, Jack and I formed an LLC called YBR Publishing. Not long after, my husband Bill signed on as our Chief Editor and Staff Manager. To date, we have published 31 books for clients (including the one in your hands now), with many more to come.

When not working on client's books, I can be found with my "lap warmer" cat, "Scooter".

www.ingramcontent.com/pod-product-compliance
Lightning Source LLC
Chambersburg PA
CBHW060459300726
48975CB00008B/2568